THE LOST SKETCHBOOK

A MODERN HISTORY MYSTERY

ADRIAN STEAD

ISBN: 978-1-7643942-0-8

Prologue

1819

'Mr Turner! Welcome to Venice. Welcome to the Palazzo Mocenigo. Have you had a good journey?'

'The journey was pleasing enough, thank you, my lord.'

'Dispense with that old fellow; just call me George.'

'And, similarly with you, sir, please call me William.'

'You will need refreshment, William. My housekeeper will find us something. Margherita ...'

An unkempt looking, but attractive woman of about twenty-two with black hair and angry dark eyes answered Lord Byron's call. He spoke to her in excellent Italian. She grunted an acknowledgement and, casting a disparaging look at Turner, exited the room.

'You will, of course, lodge with me here in my menagerie, eh? It is in a marvellous location right on the Grand Canal.'

'I do not want to intrude on your generosity, sir.'

'Bah! Of course you will stay. Archer,' who was hovering in the hallway as a good valet should, 'take Mr Turner's belongings to the green room. Now, come, sit with me, sir. I am in the midst of writing a new poem, y'know. It starts: 'I stood in Venice, on the Bridge of Sighs, A palace and a prison on each hand.' Oh, but you don't want to hear this now. I will read it to you later. Perhaps you would like to add an illustration to it when finished? We shall consider it. Now, tell me of your journey. Was it very exhausting?'

Turner and Byron, especially, spent a good while chatting about art, poetry, women, and English matters generally. 'Do make yourself at home, William. You are free to use the Palazzo as you see fit. We make no demands here. You may find us a little bohemian, but what of it, eh?' Byron smacked Turner's arm. Turner winced.

Nestled among other historic palazzi, Palazzo Mocenigo holds a prime position in one of Venice's most picturesque and vibrant areas: the Grand Canal. From its balconies, one can gaze upon the iconic Rialto Bridge, a stone's throw away and watch the daily ebb and flow of life on the canal. The gentle lapping of the water against the palazzo's foundations provided a soothing albeit decaying accompaniment to life within its walls, creating a sense of harmony and connection with the city's unique aquatic environment.

The palazzo's facade, adorned with pointed arches, intricately carved stonework, and elegant balconies, reflected the ornate style that characterises many of

Venice's historic buildings. Its rose-hued marble gleamed in the soft light of the Venetian sun, casting a warm glow enhancing its ethereal beauty. Majestic windows framed by delicate tracery overlook the bustling Grand Canal, offering a glimpse into the storied past of this enchanting edifice. An environment well-suited to the unique talents of both men.

Inside, the palazzo was a world of refined luxury and artistic splendour. The grand entrance hall, with its high ceilings and lavish frescoes, set the tone for the palatial interiors. Richly upholstered furniture, gilded mirrors, and sumptuous draperies adorned the rooms, creating an atmosphere of opulence and sophistication.

Each room was a masterpiece in itself, filled with exquisite artworks, intricate tapestries, and fine furnishings. The grand salon, where Byron entertained his guests, featured a magnificent chandelier that cast a warm, inviting glow over the room. Bookshelves lined the walls, housing an impressive collection of literary works reflecting Byron's intellectual pursuits.

The beautiful Palazzo Mocenigo was a true gem of Venetian architecture and a fitting residence for one of the most celebrated poets of the Romantic era.

When Margherita and Archer heard Turner had been granted free rein of the palazzo, they were displeased with the arrangement. They had both taken a dislike to this Englishman, whom Archer considered to be a person of low means and upbringing, exemplified by his

Cockney accent. Margherita called him 'sconcio', of a dirty disposition.

William Archer, the valet, was a married man with two children at home in London. He had begun his association with his employer in England in 1804, starting as a footman and being made valet in 1806, when the previous incumbent was sacked, tried for theft, and transported. Archer devoted himself to Byron's service and received higher pay than others in similar positions elsewhere. The overpayment, he assumed, was because of Byron's need for him to be, shall we say, discreet in what he saw, heard, and learnt about his employer.

It was Archer's intent to return to London with sufficient wealth to begin a business, making and selling Italian-style pasta products. It was a risk, he knew, as English families were loath to experiment with new, foreign foods, but he was sure he could make a good go of it.

The artist eventually took his leave of the poet and the salon, and went in search of his bedroom, inspecting the Palazzo's fine but dilapidating rooms as he went. The green room, he found, didn't look out onto the Grand Canal but to an enclosed courtyard at the rear of the building. He was keen to begin his work, so picking up a sketchbook and pencils, he headed off to find a suitable sketching spot somewhere on the Canal.

Within one week, Turner had produced four sketchbooks, comprising 160 pages, as well as four large watercolours in sketch form. But there was a further, unfinished, small sketchbook that he kept separate containing beautiful pencil drawings of the Palazzo, its various rooms and some of the Palazzo's inhabitants drawn secretly from alcoves or behind screens. He took much pleasure in secreting himself in dark areas of the palazzo to watch and to record. There were two other sketches which he drew while enjoying his voyeuristic activities. The first was in the evening, with the chandelier casting its low sparkling light over the centre of the salon, of Byron having sex with a naked Margherita, so alive and intimate one could almost smell the sweat and mess and body fluids. The other was of Byron on another evening lying naked on a couch with a young curly-haired boy, Margherita's young cousin, also unclothed, astride him. Turner found both the watching of his subjects and the resultant sketches shocking, yet exciting and stimulating.

One morning when the artist was out of the house on some errand not related to his art, Archer took the opportunity to snoop around Turner's room. His previous delving into other guests' belongings had reaped good rewards of cash and jewellery, which the brokers on the Giudecca had converted for him. He hadn't been greedy, taking only what was likely not to be missed for some time. This trait was a flaw in his otherwise professional character and would culminate in his later personal indebtedness, which would see the man in debtor's prison in the mid-1830s after the collapse of his London-based business.

Turner, however, was not a wealthy man, and Archer was disappointed to find nothing of value. There were, however, the sketchbooks, although he realised it would be difficult to lift them easily. There was a small sketchbook that he came upon in the chest of drawers. He opened it, finding beautiful sketches of the Palazzo. He thought them exquisite although he knew little of art. Then he saw the obscene drawings of his employer.

Not the sort of things the brokers dealt in, he thought, and then beamed as he recognised the female in the drawing. Margherita.

He enjoyed looking at her naked body. Archer had seen Milord countless times with many women, so seeing his nakedness was nothing to him and nothing about Lord Byron's sexual proclivities surprised him anymore, but Margherita Cogni was a different matter.

With neither he nor Margherita liking Turner or having him stay with them, he was delighted to realise that a thought had come to him of a way to have him removed and, at the same time, have some fun with the housekeeper.

With a smirk on his faced, Archer took the sketchbook and went in search of Margherita.

He found her in the kitchen preparing a meal. He placed his right hand on her buttock and squeezed. She dropped her knife in shock, slapped Archer hard across his left cheek and yelled what he assumed were obscenities at him. He merely laughed, and still grinning, produced the sketchbook for her to see.

What she screeched next when she saw the sketch of her with Byron Archer had no idea, even though he spoke passable Italian, but the raving and thrashing of arms made it clear to him what she felt.

Still laughing, Archer did his best to placate her. 'Reste calmo, prego. Calm down, please. Please.' He put his arms around her to try to halt her frenetic rantings, and eventually, she gave in to his ministrations but continued to mutter obscenities now aimed at the artist into his chest.

'Margherita, listen, we can rid ourselves of this dirty man. When he returns to the palazzo later today, and Milord is out of the building, we will confront him and order him to leave or face the wrath of Milord when we show him what he has been doing in our home.'

Margherita was satisfied with the proposal.

And this is what they did, leaving Turner with no option but to do as they commanded. Embarrassed, he left them immediately. 'I shall send for my things when I have arranged new lodgings. My sketchbook, if you please.'

'No, sir, the book stays with Signora Cogni as surety against any deceit or falsehood that may chance to happen.'

'How do you mean, by that?'

'Should you choose to deny your hand in this matter and defame either or both of us.'

Turner protested vehemently but to no avail. Frustratedly, he left the room and the palazzo. Archer and Margherita smiled at each other in satisfaction at their complicity. Margherita kept the sketchbook secret.

Upon his return, Lord Byron showed indifference to Turner's departure when told. 'It is as it is,' was all he said about it. 'I have other things to concern me.'

Three weeks later, Byron left Margherita and Venice for Ravenna with a 21-year-old Countess Guiccioli; Archer went with him.

'Milord, George, dear heart, you cannot go. You cannot leave me. Not for her! Do not do this to me. Stay, oh please stay.' Margherita's pleas fell on deaf ears. Byron had had enough of her and had found another new love.

Her pleas changed to threats. 'I will kill you rather than let you go.' She ran to the kitchen and produced a large knife. 'You will be sorry. I shall kill you!'

She put up a terrible scene, but Byron wrestled the knife from her. In hysterics, she rushed from the room, from the palazzo and hurled herself screaming into the Canal. Archer, however, was at hand to fish her out unscathed, and he took her to her bedroom, while she screamed and wailed wretchedly all the way.

In complete misery, Margherita had no choice but to pack her meagre belongings, including the sketchbook, and return to a loveless marriage with her husband, Giorgio Cogni and her 6-year-old son, Francesco.

Five years later, in 1824, Byron died while in Greece, having moved there from Ravenna via Genoa with Countess Guiccioli. She would leave him, however, one year before his death.

In 1843, Margherita's son Francesco married and opened a pensione in a calle in San Polo close to the Rialto Bridge on the Grand Canal. Giorgio had died by this time, and when Margherita also died, in 1845, her son rescued her clothes and other items and stored them in a wooden box in the pensione's attic. There they remained, forgotten, as the business passed to grandson Lorenzo and finally to great-grandson Alessandro in 1922, at the age of forty-one.

Alessandro was forced to close the pensione at the outset of the Second World War, moving his family out of Venice to Milan, where his married daughter Giulia was living with her husband, Gianluca Rossi, as the fascists began taking control of Serenissima. In 1948, Alessandro returned to Venice, dying there in 1950.

The pensione building had stood empty throughout the war and afterwards until 1958, when new tenants – no relations - began clearing everything from the building to enable modernisation. The sketchbook, then not in the best of condition outwardly, was found by the new tenants sometime later when they were clearing out the attic and only cursorily glanced at before being taken to a second-hand bookseller to be disposed of in September 1960.

Guido Zampelli's second-hand bookstore could be found close to Rio Marin in the Santa Croce area of Venice. Like the city it was in, it was old, falling down, disorganised, yet still functional and packed with accumulated wonder. It had once been a vaulted storage cellar with green double doors opening out onto the piazza. The only natural light came from the doors being open – natural air conditioning Guido called it. He shared this cornucopia with Dante, a contented, all-knowing tabby cat that basked in the superiority of being, probably, of the lineage of those cats responsible for saving the city from the plague back in the fourteenth century.

It was only a short while after Guido had acquired the store that the cat had strolled in and announced to Guido that he was staying.

A good omen thought Guido. *He looks like a Dante to me, so that's what I'll call him.*

Dante had complete disregard for those human customers who visited his store. He had his favourite books on which to sleep – English novels for some reason being particularly preferred – and woe betide anyone that tried to shift him to get at a book or two.

And books were everywhere. Wherever Guido could find space to store them, he did. To the casual customer, there appeared to be no logic to their positioning, but Guido knew what was where – mostly!

Trestle tables creaked and groaned under the weight of Venetian and World History; ramshackle shelves teemed with foreign language books; the floor was carpeted at various parts of the store with both fiction and non-fiction; even the stairs to the upper floor's art and literature section were piled high with travel and gastronomy items.

Guido loved being a bookseller. Venetian by birth, he had, in his earlier life, been a sommelier in one of Venice's premier hotel restaurants. He had loved the work, but the hours had been long, and while most of the customers had been a pleasure to serve, more and more were becoming loud, ignorant, and obnoxious to the extent that as he got older, he was finding it increasingly hard to remain pleasant to his customers and contented in his duties. So, when his wife tragically died, he, at the age of forty-eight, changed his lifestyle, and opened his bookstore.

Guido had done what he could to nurse his wife through her illness and make her world as comfortable as it could be, but cancer is no friend to anyone, and, in the end, he was relieved that she would not be suffering as she had in the last twelve months of her life. He was stoic throughout this period, and his attitude to life became, not unsurprisingly, quieter and more introspective. It was over a year before he could enjoy life again through his store and interaction with his lovely customers.

Guido had bought the bookstore from a woman who had found its upkeep too much for her aging body, and it took him many weeks to get some order into the place before he could introduce his own stock and give it some sense of organisation.

The delicious smell of old books – that dusty, vanillin aroma – mingled with the musty earthiness of old stone and plaster, so evocative of times past, pervaded the store. For a man who had such knowledge of aromas from his association with wine, the store's frowstiness was immensely comforting, like a bottle of old, quality Burgundy.

Into this world, Turner's old and battered sketchbook came one late Monday afternoon in September 1960.

When one of the new owners of the pensione in San Polo brought the sketchbook to Guido's store, she was oblivious to its contents other than that there were 'a few nice drawings of rooms and buildings in there.' Its tan cloth cover was in poor condition: grimy, discoloured, and stained.

At the time of her arrival at the front counter, Guido was being rushed off his feet by six American tourists seeking advice about books on Venice. He saw her there and held his hand up in acknowledgement.

'My husband and I thought you might like this,' she called, holding the item up for the bookseller to see. 'We thought it should go somewhere where it could be appreciated.'

'Sorry, I didn't quite hear you.'

'Excuse me,' one of the tourists said, 'what about this book? Does it show where ...'

'Hey! Look at this one. Is this any good?'

Guido was doing his best to respond to their questions and was conscious of the need to help the woman at the front counter.

'I am sorry, Signorina, I'll be with you in a moment.'

'Oh, sorry, I can see you're busy. Shall I leave it at the cash register?'

'This book's got maps. Are they accurate, do you know?' One of the tourists thrust the open book at Guido.

'Yes, I think so.' 'Signorina, would you mind dropping it onto that table, there?' Guido pointed the woman in the direction of a crowded table near an alcove. 'I'll get to you in a moment'

'How much is this book? Is it original?'

These customers kept Guido busy for some time. He was perversely grateful that no other customer was in his shop seeking his attention, and after the tourists had left, happy with their purchases, he was weary but returned his thoughts to the woman with her item, but she had left, so he decided to close up and go for a grappa at the nearby bar.

Chapter One

Robert Ferngrove was an honest young man. That is, until JMW Turner's sketchbook, which contained indecent and explicit drawings of Lord Byron from their time together in Venice, came into his possession. That's when his life changed irreparably.

~

July 1961

'My God, Robert, just look at this place!' Jonathan Spencer's eyes flew around bookshelves, tables, the floor, boxes. Books poured out in front of him: large books, small books, fat books, thin books, books of colour; age battered and glossy new. Higgledy-piggledy. A collision of worlds, all in this one small shop.

'It's amazing,' Jonathan continued. 'It's crying out for me to just dive headfirst into it all.'

'Steady on.' Robert's quiet sense of propriety always found it difficult for him to contain Jonathan's passionate excess when excited. 'I think we should take our time to have a good look around. We need to do this methodically.'

'Oh, you and your method and logic,' Jonathan teased, stroking Robert's bare left forearm just below the cuff of his cream short-sleeved cotton shirt, 'but I expect you're right. Where should we start?'

The two men stepped off the stone threshold of the wide-open, green, double-doored entrance into the duskiness of Guido's shop, made dark by the glare of an afternoon sun that pounded the campo behind them. They waited a moment for their eyes to fully adjust to this welcoming coolness and shade. A woman's high-pitched laugh reverberated somewhere in the August heat behind them. A Venetian laugh. There weren't too many tourists that visited this campo, set well away from the pulsating Piazza San Marco.

'It's beautifully chaotic.' Jonathan enthused.

'Actually, Jon, if you look carefully, you'll find that there is order here. The hand-written cards delineating the sections of shelves that announce subject matters and the books within those sections.'

'Oh, yes, you're right. Someone must have spent a lot of time and love doing them all.'

Six other men and two women shared this space with them. Four were in unintentional poses of reverence, standing, head bowed, and eyes transfixed on whatever universes were pulling them in between the covers of the items in their hands.

'Bondi, benvegnuo.' A man approached them. 'Venesian?'

'No, Inglese.' Robert responded.

'Ah, welcome. My English is not good, but you can like my shop please.'

'Grazi, we will.' Robert smiled.

The man gave a courteous nod and melted back into the fabric of the shop.

'I think I'll start over here,' Jonathan pointed to the stairs housing piles of travel and gastronomy books, 'and move on up the stairs. I think I see art books at the top!'

'Then I'll start where that cat is.'

'What cat?' asked Jonathan.

Robert pointed to tables on the opposite side of the room to where Jonathan was about to head. It was a shame that Robert was unaware of the cat's name, given his adoration of The Divine Comedy. Did Dante cast an acknowledging glance at Robert, or did Robert merely imagine it?

Robert Ferngrove and Jonathan Spencer both loved visiting second-hand book shops – a sort of busman's holiday, Jonathan had said – looking for stock for their own bookshop. An occupational pleasure even while on holiday.

They had acquired the lease on 26 Cecil Court, London, WC2 on 8 October 1960 after they had left Oxford University. They had often talked about running a bookshop while they were both at Oxford. It was one of those 'one-day' dreams they shared. They spent many happy hours cozied up in one or the other's room, chatting about where the shop would be, how to finance it, stock and so on. To find the dream in the prestigious location of Cecil Court elevated it beyond their most optimistic hopes.

Cecil Court is a hidden gem nestled in the heart of bustling, smoke-filled London, a haven for bibliophiles and history buffs. A 300-foot-long pedestrian thoroughfare with Charing Cross Road and its myriad book and music shops at one end and St Martins Lane and its theatres at the other. The court is full of Victorian-era shopfronts draped in ironwork and adorned with hanging signs aligning it. The scent of aged paper and leather beckons from open doors. At the time of them taking the lease, over twenty-four bookshops and print dealers offered their fine wares: glorious first editions, dusty tomes, children's classics, and old maps from sagging shelves and proud displays. Here, perhaps, a visitor may have found time standing still while strolling the flagstones, picking up books randomly and feeling their magic, then wondering at the colourful cartography that caught the senses.

And if that visitor were to close their eyes and listen, they might have heard a faint echo of one of Mozart's melodies, whispering and dancing amidst the cobbles of the court. They would then be in 1764, with a young Wolfgang Amadeus Mozart practising his keyboard exercises before sliding into one of his compositions. The beautiful music touching the damp, warm air. Or would the visitor have heard the eight-year-old prodigy clattering through the Court, laughing raucously, his eyes sparkling with fun and childish intent, down from a three-bedroomed apartment on the first floor above the barber shop in the court and out towards surprised walkers along St Martins Lane? The boisterousness and abandonment infectious on those who witnessed the spectacle, just as in a little while, he would astound audiences at nearby Haymarket and Spring Gardens concerts with his precocious talent. Cecil Court was a humble backdrop for such genius.

The shop at Number 26 was in poor condition when Robert and Jonathan took the lease. They spent quite some time installing better shelving and lighting before stocking it with good quality books and artwork, which they acquired gradually from auctions and deceased estate purchases around the country.

It had taken a few months for the shop to become an established part of the court. Robert's knowledge of literature, especially Italian and classical literature, enabled the shop to display beautiful editions, including an early print of Dante's Divine Comedy, of which Robert was particularly proud. There were sets of Cicero, Livy, Ovid, and Marcus Aurelius as well as early English writers and, as a nod to modernism, children's classics such as those by Enid Blyton, CS Lewis, Beatrix Potter, and Kenneth Grahame, oh, and of course, Rupert Bear annuals dating from 1937. Robert's Oxford-induced love of Byron and The Romantics featured prominently, too, especially the former, where many early editions were to be found, as well as biographies and histories.

Jonathan's experience of art history enabled some spectacular prints and art books to be included in the shop. Both loved Turner, Monet, and The Impressionists, so their books and prints abounded too.

They were fortunate to have had parents who assisted them financially at the outset of their London days. This, however, did not last for Robert. When he had visited his parents' home near Bristol in the Autumn of 1960, he told them how he had met Jonathan, about how they spent a lot of time together, his love for him and about his sexual feelings. His father's reaction to these revelations shocked Robert completely. He had no idea that the man he had always revered and respected all his life would be so hostile to this news. His son's 'perversion' horrified and repulsed Mr Ferngrove. There were much condemnation and harsh words said. Robert's father had even stormed out of the room at one stage. It was his mother who expressed the understanding and concern for Robert that he had hoped for and, indeed, expected from them both. His father's reaction bitterly disappointed him and left him in tears. From then on, there was a significant rift between them which never abated.

Robert found out at a later date that his father's revulsion was accompanied by a fear of being discovered as the father of a heinous criminal, even allowing for the Wolfenden Report, which recommended to the British Government that homosexuality should be made legal. Alan Ferngrove was scared that information about his son would 'get out' and cause him problems with his bank employers.

So, the financial support Robert had received at university and shortly afterwards ended. Thankfully, Jonathan's resources were sufficient for them to rent a two-bedroom flat on Ufford Street, Southwark, South of the City. They moved in together and were happy there. But it was 1961; they had to remain discreet about their home arrangements and not attract unwanted attention. They succeeded in keeping themselves private.

They had given their shop a thorough clean and re-equipping of the interior before placing the valuable stock on show. They had worked strenuously and were proud of their efforts and the items they displayed. This break of a week in Venice was well-earned and much needed, though Robert had been a little reluctant to leave the shop, even in the hands of his more-than-capable younger sister, Joanna.

Being careful not to disturb the cat, Robert wound his way around stacked tables and shelves, dipping occasionally into books that caught his fancy either through colour, title, or age, while Jonathan moved upstairs into a small area housing his particular loves, forever hopeful of finding a gem of an art book or a fascinating history of a style or artist. That was, however, rare, and today did not prove to be any different. He wasn't despondent though, befitting his usual happy approach to life.

Descending the stairs, he lovingly watched Robert moving slowly toward him, gazing at spines on shelves and old tables of magazines and assorted books. He was carrying a book.

'Found something?' asked Jonathan as they came together near a small alcove.

'Yes, it's nothing especially exciting, but I haven't come across this edition before.' Robert passed the book to Jonathan.

'Marcus Aurelius. Meditations.' Jonathan opened the book with care. 'In Latin. Translation by Schultz, 1802. Is it for the shop?'

'Yes, I think so. It will need a little cleaning up first, though. I'll find out the price.'

Jonathan handed the book back to Robert, but as he did so, bumped the small table they were standing next to, and books and magazines slid to the floor.

'Damn!'

They crouched down to gather up the items and replace them on the table. A slim, battered, old cloth-covered book caught Jonathan's attention. He opened it casually and stood up, agape at what he saw.

'What's the matter?' asked Robert.

'Look. A drawing. And another,' turning over the page. 'And another. The book's not in great condition, but you know what? I rather think the drawings have the quality of Turner. See that interior sketch? It has all his characteristics: energy and immediacy of the moment. We simply have to buy it so we can examine it in more detail.'

They took the two items to the counter by the front entrance. From nowhere, seemingly, the man who had greeted them upon their arrival appeared at their sides.

'Hello. You have liked my shop?'

'Yes, most definitely. You have some wonderful books,' said Robert.

'Thank you. You are buying this one?'

'Yes. How much is it, please?'

'It is five thousand lira.'

'What's that in pounds, Robert?' asked Jonathan.

'About two pounds, sixteen and eight.' Robert announced after a struggle with the mental calculation.

'That's pretty good value. We should be able to make a profit on that, shouldn't we?'

'After I've had a good look at restoring it. And how much for this, please?' Robert handed the shop owner, Guido, the old sketchbook.

Guido looked perplexed and tried to remember where this had come from, but he couldn't.

'I do not know this,' said Guido as he examined the cover, front and back, and wasn't impressed with it. 'Five hundred lira?'

'Are you sure?'

'Yes, take it. I do not want this thing in my shop.'

So, they did just that, paying Guido with a traveller's cheque.

'Mmm, thank you. Take also my card. Tell your friends in England come see me when they visit our beautiful city.'

'We will, Senore … Zampelli.' Then, after a moment's hesitation, Robert continued. 'We, too, are booksellers. In London. Here is my card. He fished one from his wallet. We would be interested in buying old books from Venetian writers. At the right price, of course. Would you be interested in letting us know about any you find?'

'Of course,' Guido beamed.

'If any come into your possession, please write to me with the details, and we would look to purchase them.'

'It will be an honour to do so. Thank you, sir. Please write your names and address of your shop in my order book here.'

Guido pointed to the spot, and Robert inserted the relevant information.

'It has been a pleasure meeting with you, Mr Ferngrove. I will be in contact.'

The day was still hot as they headed out of the shop and readjusted their eyes to the glare. A trattoria with seats and tables under a green awning in the campo beckoned them for a cool drink, but they ignored the call and headed off down the tight calle that would take them to the Rialto Bridge, the throng of tourists, and, just beyond, their hotel.

They were keen to get along, unlike the sauntering stroll they had made on the way to discovering the bookstore. It had been a fabulous find and quite unexpected. They had crossed over a small footbridge that tethered itself precariously to the corners of four dilapidated buildings and that spanned – a generous term – the small canal, and there it appeared, on the left. Books on stands abutting the exterior wall and a large opening that would, upon closing, house a not-so-solid-looking door.

Tourist traffic gradually began flooding toward them as they apologetically wound their way through the tramp of hot bodies. The buildings on each side of the various calles afforded some shade, but the heat still permeated the air. Nor was there relief when they reached Campo San Cassiano, the route continuing at its far side.

The closer the Rialto Bridge came, the greater the heave of bodies, now heading in a multitude of directions making headway even slower. But upon reaching the Venetian icon of the Rialto, the pulse of bodies became streamlined, albeit still slow, almost carrying Robert and

Jonathan up past the gaudy and expensive shops, over the peak, and down the other side.

A few minutes more and they were at their hotel.

There weren't many hotels in Venice offering connecting bedrooms, and they had chosen the appropriately named Splendido Hotel because of its central location close to both the Grand Canal and St Mark's Square. And because Robert had stayed there once before on the recommendation of a friend and had found it comfortable, considerate, and convenient.

Jonathan had pronounced the hotel 'delightful' and was quite childlike in his excitement at arriving in a sleek taxi launch from the newly built Marco Polo airport to the hotel's front docking area.

The connecting rooms, used mainly for families, were important for Robert and Jonathan to maintain their need for discretion in their activities. Italy was, after all, a Catholic country. The hotel provided a first-rate restaurant, a lovely lounge area, and a roof terrace that Jonathan especially found 'gorgeous'.

In Robert's room, with cold drinks in hand, they kicked off their shoes and sat in the leather, high-backed chairs around the coffee table and began examining their purchases, Jonathan slowly and carefully turning the pages of the sketchbook.

'Robert, these sketches really could be Turner's, you know.'

'You're the art expert, Jon. Do you really think so?'

'I do. They are remarkably good and have all the makings of his work, and he actually visited Venice at least twice in his lifetime. Look at these interiors.'

He held the book out to Robert.

'They are magnificent,' Robert agreed.

Jonathan turned more pages, looking intently at each one.

'Oh lor, oh my!' He had reached the sketch of what was clearly Byron having sex with a woman. 'Robert, look. Look!'

Robert looked. What he saw astounded him.

'My God! Is that who I think it is? Is it Byron? If it is and this truly is Turner's work, we've come across something really special and highly controversial. Very rare. Can you be sure, Jon?'

'I don't know, Robert. I'll have to take the book to a Turner expert back home, but I'm pretty sure.'

'Oh, Christ!' Jonathan had turned another page to reveal Byron again in a debauched pose with a young boy. 'Jesus!'

'What is it?'

With mouth agape, Jonathan passed the book again to Robert.

'That is Byron, isn't it? But it's so, so ...' Words failed him.

'Yes, it is, isn't it?'

They gave a long look at each other.

'Turn the page, Robert. What else is there?'

'Nothing. It's blank. And so is the next one, and the next. That's the last drawing.'

They both sat staring at nothing in particular as the enormity of their find sank in. Jonathan's fingers had gone to his mouth, while Robert looked vacantly out of the window to the balcony across the small canal. The book still in his hand. He felt light-headed, euphoric almost. And he had a strange sense of connection and intimacy with it.

'I need a gin and tonic.' Jonathan, at last, announced.

'What? Oh yes, what a good idea.' His reverie over.

'Come on, let's go down to the bar and find a quiet corner and consider what we're going to do about this.'

Leaving the sketchbook on the coffee table, Robert locked the door, and they moved downstairs.

Drinks in hand and heads conspiratorially close together, the two of them sought answers to their own questions. Namely:

'Can we identify the locations that are the drawings' subjects?'

'Can we date the sketchbook?'

'Is the book from England?'

'Will the type of paper give us an idea of its origin?'

'Should we try to find an expert on Turner's work for authentication purposes?'

'What are the ramifications if we show it to a third party?'

'Can we keep this to ourselves? Indeed, should we?'

Jonathan glanced almost furtively at the bar, where two other guests sat, and in lowered tones, said, 'There's an awful lot to consider, Robert.'

'I think, Jon, that we need to approach it all systematically. There is no doubt that the drawings are of buildings along the Grand Canal, mostly. Then, there are others of interiors with people, excluding the two 'interesting ones', shall we say! I think we should try to locate these buildings, if possible, over the remaining couple of days that we have left here.'

'Yes, I agree.'

'We also should go with your instincts and expertise as an art historian, Jon, and trust that the sketchbook belonged to Turner. That may help us locate where the interiors are. It has to be Byron in those drawings.'

Jonathan nodded in agreement. 'Most certainly.'

'So, we must assume that the sketches were of Byron's residence here in Venice. That has to be our starting point. I'm sure the concierge here can tell us where Byron lived.'

The concierge knew. 'Yes, the Lord Byron stayed at Palazzo Mocenigo on the Grand Canal, nearer to St Mark's Square than we are. But I am sorry to say that the Palazzo is now owned by the civic authorities here in Venice and is not open to the public. I can show you on this map.'

The news came as a great disappointment to the two men.

'You can see the building from the vaporetto that passes it, right here.' The concierge pointed to the location, and Robert and Jonathan followed his finger.

So, they determined to keep the sketchbook safe in Robert's room and enjoy the rest of their Venetian stay before departing for home in three days' time. They spent the intervening time as tourists, resignedly viewing the Palazzo exterior on their way to St Mark's Square, visiting the Doge's Palace, the Basilica, and, importantly for Jonathan, the Galleria dell 'Accademia. They wined and dined well, but the sketchbook, forever present in Robert's mind, pulled at him, constantly.

'I don't want to put the book in the shop, Jon.' Robert said, not wanting to face Jonathan with the announcement. 'Will you be alright with that?'

'Why ever not? It could be worth a fortune.'

'I know. I know we've talked about this in Venice, but even now, on the plane home, I can't stop thinking about it. I can't let it go.'

'Robert, you know I'm unsure about this. We could make a good profit that could set us up for years, possibly.'

'I understand that, Jon, but I just can't bring myself to part with it.'

'But Robert ...'

'No.'

'What if we were to donate it to a museum or public gallery? We could have our names linked to it that way. It would be good publicity for the shop.'

'No!' Robert snapped the response. 'Sorry, but no. I must have it.'

Robert realised his aggression had taken Jonathan aback. He wasn't normally like that, being such a placid man, a trait which he knew Jonathan loved and envied about him. He was conscious that his response would have puzzled and upset his partner and was sad that it would have done.

'You're not sulking, are you, Jon?' he asked a few moments later.

'Jon?'

'We'll talk about this again later, Robert.' Jonathan said quietly.

For the rest of the journey, little more passed between them.

As the taxi pulled up outside the block of their Southwark flat, they were glad to be back, but the conversation on the plane had taken the edge off Jonathan's happiness. It wouldn't be the last time, either.

Chapter Two

'Jon, I'm sorry if I hurt your feelings back there on the plane. You know I wouldn't do that intentionally.'

Robert looked appealingly at his partner. While he wouldn't wittingly hurt this beautiful young man, he knew that sometimes, if he was honest with himself, he could be a little over-protective, which could be construed as being controlling. He never meant to of course and he truly did feel remorse when it occurred to him that he had behaved that way in the past. He had loved Jonathan from their first meeting when he gazed in wonder at his hair of copper and a face an angel would be jealous of.

Robert had first become conscious of not finding girls particularly attractive at around age fourteen, although he did enjoy their company, especially when talking about the boys at school. This latent homosexuality didn't manifest itself fully until he reached university in Oxford. At fourteen, however, his feelings caused him much confusion, and he worried about not being 'normal'. Fear of persecution by school colleagues and teachers and the possibility of rejection by family and his community began to concern him, but not to the extent that he became depressed and alone. He did have friends of similar orientation but wondered whether their mutual gratifications were merely a stage in his life that he would grow out of. There was no one seemingly he could talk to about his feelings. Certainly not his father, nor the school or church pastors. He wasn't sure about whether he could confide in his mother. Instead, he tried to ignore his urges and concentrated on his schoolwork and love of literature.

Upon finding his feet at Oxford, the level of homosexual activity happening in his college, Magdalen, opened Robert's eyes. With a great deal of trepidation, he allowed himself to participate in the many university activities that brought him into contact with other homosexual students, and while closeted within the walls of academia, he embraced the society of like-minded men. He didn't interact exclusively with gay men, but Jonathan was different. It was love at first sight. It was love still.

'I don't want to talk about it right now, Robert. I'm tired. It's been a long journey back from Venice, and you know that things coming to an end don't sit well with me, holidays particularly. Let's just go to bed. We'll talk more in the morning.'

At 7 a.m., Robert opened the bedroom curtains to a grey and soddened South London sky. The dull and grimy brickwork of the buildings opposite did not help the greyness. He sighed and trooped into the bathroom while Jonathan sat up in bed, waiting his turn to use it and giving him time to think.

When they were both washed, brushed, and dressed, they undertook their normal chores in the kitchen before sitting down to breakfast. Robert focused on spooning sugar into Jonathan's tea. The spoon tinkled against the mug, the sound exacerbated by the silence that still hung in the room. To Robert's relief, Jonathan broke the silence completely.

'Robert, I've been thinking about how we can get the sketchbook authenticated.'

'Oh. How?' Robert was pleased that Jonathan's demeanour seemed happier again.

'You remember Stuart, who opened his bookbinding business with his father?'

'Yes, I think so.'

'Well, the old man was a bit of a whizz on old binding methods. He could probably help us out and date the sketchbook binding?'

'I'm not sure that's a good idea.'

'Why ever not?'

'It would mean showing him the sketches and ...'

'No, no, it wouldn't. I've thought about that last night.'

'Oh, Jon, I'm sorry. Did you not sleep well?'

'I'm fine, darling, really. No, I was thinking; there are blank pages at the back of the book. He would look at those, not the sketches.' Jonathan was getting excited again. 'And he can see the cover and the binding! I'm sure it will be fine. And they're in Mitcham, not far away from Mother in Wimbledon. I need to catch up with her, so could do the two things at the same time. What d'you say?'

'Possibly.' Robert drew the word out hesitatingly. 'When do you want us to do it?'

'Well, today, I thought.'

'Today! What about the shop? Joanna will expect us back today. There'll be so much to catch up on.'

'Well, you go to the shop, and I'll go see Mother and take the sketchbook to Stuart's.'

The thought of the sketchbook being out of his possession horrified Robert, the ghosts of lending a prized book to a supposed friend years ago and never getting it back painfully reared their heads again. 'But you'll be on the train and in public. You could be robbed. What then?'

'Robert, calm down. No need to panic. I'll take good care of it. It'll be alright.'

'Can't we do this some other time together?'

'Yes, of course, we can, but I just thought seeing Mother and being so close to Mitcham would be a good opportunity to find out about the book for sure.'

The arrangement was frightful to Robert, but it did make sense to him to verify the book's origins if Stuart's father could do so. Just the thought of the book leaving his keeping was unnerving, and Jonathan had had problems with losing things in the past, hadn't he? Hadn't he?

'How will you get there?'

'I'll take a taxi from here to Waterloo, then get the train to Earlsfield, as I have before, then take another taxi to Mother's on Whatmore Street. Then, it's only a short taxi ride from there to Mitcham. You know that'

'Well, that sounds alright. What will you do when you've finished in Mitcham?'

'I'll get another taxi to Tooting Broadway and come straight up on the Northern line to Leicester Square. I should be with you in the shop just about lunchtime if I head off now.'

Robert tried desperately to allow himself to be happy to agree to the plan, and it was only seeing Jonathan's excitement that he realised he couldn't disappoint him again.

'Álright, but for God's sake, be careful.'

Robert wondered whether his anxiety was for Jonathan's well-being or for that of the sketchbook, but didn't reach a satisfactory conclusion, which worried him less than it ought.

'I'll put it in the leather briefcase.'

Robert removed the book from the sideboard drawer, where he had placed it the night before and deposited it into the briefcase, which Joanathan produced from the bedroom.

'Are you sure you'll be all right doing this?'

'Yes, of course. Stop fretting. I'll be fine.'

Robert shared the taxi to Waterloo with Jonathan, shaking hands, rather than their usual private kiss on the cheek, at the station before saying farewell with Jonathan and his precious cargo heading off to the ticket office of the South West Trains company and Robert hesitatingly going for the tube to take him to Leicester Square and the short walk to Cecil Court and their shop.

Robert always took great pride in seeing 'Ferngrove and Spencer' over their business premises and this morning was no different.

'Hello Robbie, welcome back. How was Venice? Where's Jonathan?' Joanna was chirpy and clearly pleased to see her brother as he came into the shop.

'Hello, darling, thank you.' There was no one in the shop, so it was safe to give his sister a kiss. 'We had a wonderful time and made what we believe is an absolutely super find, which I'll tell you about in a moment. In fact, that's why Jon's not with me; he's on a mission regarding it and will be here later.'

'Sounds intriguing.'

'Yes, but more of that later. Pop the kettle on, and you can tell me what's been going on here.'

A small area at the back of the shop, away from the public gaze, created by Robert and Jonathan, housed a small kitchen with a gas ring, kettle and hooks on the side of a bookcase where cups hung. Standing on top of a tiny storage cupboard in which tea, milk, biscuits, and cutlery lay hidden away by a curtain was a space for making their drinks. Two stools comprised the seating facilities.

With the teapot and their cups replete, Joanna filled Robert in on how she had fared in his absence. 'I made six sales.' she proudly announced. 'The three-volume Tenant of Wildfell Hall to a lovely couple from Yorkshire, in town for a bit of a holiday. They liked to chat and were here quite a while. A delightful American woman bought the Elizabethan love poems and is also looking to have several special editions, including De Tocqueville's Journey to America, sent to her in New York if you can find them. She's left a list and her contact details. I said you'd follow it up on your return. That should keep you busy! Two Beatrix Potters were sold to customers on separate days. And, finally, the 1928 Dante, in Italian, was bought yesterday by a man.

'Well, that's brilliant. Marvellous, in fact. Thank you so much for helping out.'

'My pleasure. I'd be happy to continue for a bit longer if you'd like. Got nothing better to do.'

'No joy with getting placed yet, then?'

'No, not yet, I'm sorry to say. It just seems so bloody unfair. I can't even wangle an audition. All the orchestras are just so man driven. I've written off to Bournemouth and Hallé, but I'm not holding my breath. Lucy and I – you remember my violin-playing flatmate? – we've even thought about starting our own chamber orchestra, but it's so hard to get anything like that off the ground. I'd like to stay in London, but I don't know if I can. I've even thought about going overseas, but they're even worse than England. What is the obsession with bloody men? It seems I'm being driven into teaching. That's not what I studied for, and, ooh, I get so frustrated.' Joanna unclenched her fists, picked up her cup and sipped her tea.

Robert picked up the anger signals clearly and felt really sorry for her. 'Of course, you can stay on here if you want. We can only pay you a commission on sales, but you're welcome.'

'Thank you, Robert. That's nice of you. I do like it here in Cecil Court. Your neighbours are really friendly, and some of the stuff they sell is fabulous. Now, what's your news?'

'Venice was excellent. We had a couple of rooms at a super hotel and saw lots of things. Mostly touristy, of course. Except, we stumbled across an old bookshop where we found something quite incredible, we think. An old sketchbook. Hang on, the shop owner gave me his card.' Robert extracted it from his wallet. 'Guido Zampelli. Look. I'll pin it to the board here.'

'I bought an Aurelius' Meditation. It needs a bit of work, but it will be an excellent addition to the shop. See?' He fished it out of his bag.

Joanna handled the object lightly. 'Hmm, I think you're right about it needing a little cleaning up. Where's the sketchbook, and what makes it so special?'

'Jonathan's got it. He's taking it to someone he knows who, hopefully, can answer a few questions about it. We think it's earth-shattering if we're right. He's also going to see his mother, and to be honest, I'm very nervous about him wandering around with it.'

'I'm sure he'll be all right. You shouldn't fret so much. So, what exactly is so special about it?'

'You'll see, when it gets here.'

'Gosh, you can be so secretive when you want to, big brother.' She sipped her tea.

There were no customers at the shop that morning. The grey heaviness that hung over the capital seemingly keeping any passing traffic in the court to a gloomy minimum. And like the weather, time, too, seemed weighed down as it dragged along.

One o'clock came and went, and no sign of Jonathan. There was still no sign of him at one-thirty. Robert kept looking at the door and his wristwatch, his anxiety making him feel uncomfortable and now worried.

'Where is he?' He muttered aloud but quietly to himself. 'Where is he?'

At one-thirty-five, precisely, the door opened, and Robert watched Jonathan casually enter the shop. 'Where the hell have you been? We thought something may have happened to you!'

'We? Is Joanna still here? Oh, yes. Hello, Joanna.' Jonathan gave her a wave, and she gave him one of her genuine smiles back from the rear of the shop.

'For God's sake, Jon, you're late getting back.'

'Yes, I know, sorry, but mother wanted to know everything about the holiday, so I had to explain where we'd been, where we'd stayed, everything. She gets lonely, you know, so enjoys my visits. There was a delay in getting away. I say, have you had lunch? I'm famished. Can we pop out to the café in the Lane?'

Tree-lined Whitworth Street, Wimbledon, was where Jonathan had lived all his life before going to university. He grew up playing in the street outside his bay-fronted and gable-roofed terraced house with its small, walled front garden. The long street comprised houses of very similar construction, both internally and externally, all exuding an air of middle-class, suburban respectability, which reflected the characteristics of their inhabitants.

Mrs Spencer continued to live in the house after her husband didn't return home from the war. Mr Spencer had left her reasonably cared for financially, which for Jonathan meant he could attend a decent grammar school and gain his qualifications for university. Mrs Spencer, as if compensating for the loss of her Harold, gave her son considerable love and was extremely protective of him and keen to ensure he didn't mix with the 'wrong sort'.

Because of this devotion, the young Jonathan was a shy boy and didn't fit in particularly well with his contemporaries. He was quiet and studious but happy. Probably because of the doting he received, he carried what one auntie referred to as 'puppy fat', which stayed with him to an extent throughout his teens and early adult life.

Small, with a pale complexion and thick ginger hair, Robert Ferngrove, at university, found him quite alluring, looking younger than his years, and they quickly became friends. When it began, the sexuality of the friendship baffled Jonathan. The only close affection he had experienced was from his mother, so having close physical contact with another person, irrespective of gender, he found pleasing. He enjoyed having his hair stroked and his hand held, and when in the quiet of his room, Robert had unbuttoned his shirt and then moved his hands over his body, he felt an excitement that caught his breath. But that was nothing compared to the ecstasy he felt when Robert kissed him on the mouth and the body connection that followed.

When the physical activity was temporarily finished, Jonathan knew he wanted to get close to Robert. They spent a lot of time together and made plans for the future for them both.

'Are you able to hold the shop, Joanna, if Jon and I go to ...'

'Yes, of course. I've had my sandwiches, so I'm fine.'

'Thanks. We won't be long.'

'Did you have any luck with your friend?' Robert asked as they strolled along to the Lane Café just around the corner from the east end of the court.

'I did, yes. I'll give you the gen when we're in the café.'

The lunchtime traffic was easing off as they sat at a table in the popular eating establishment. The waitress took their order, and Jonathan related what had occurred with Stuart's father, Tom. 'He took me upstairs to what I suppose is his office, and I explained we had acquired an old sketchbook and were looking to have its age determined. I produced the book, and, as we had agreed, I opened it at a blank page toward the end of the book. Tom took the book from me and examined the paper and the binding. He held a page up to the light and scrutinised it for some minutes. He then returned to his desk.'

'Well,' he began, 'the paper is not made of wood pulp, which dates it to the mid-nineteenth century. Paper made in the eighteenth century, up to about 1820, was laid paper. It was a mesh of wires, like ribbing, when it had been laid on a rack to dry. You can see this when the paper is held up to the light. Come see at the window.'

'I did as Tom suggested, and we both looked at the page and, sure enough, there was a grid pattern present. He pointed out that there were no watermarks or other embossments to be seen so that suggested the paper was older than eighteen-forty, seemingly.'

'Also,' he continued back at his desk, 'the pages are stitched together, not glued, so once again, that dates the book as older than about the eighteen twenties. The cover of the book is interesting, too, but I'm no expert on cloth and pigments, and can only conclude that the cover complements what I have said about the paper. Does that help you?'

'So,' I asked him, nodding, 'if I said that I thought it may have belonged to the artist Turner, would that be unrealistic?'

'Turner, eh? No, not unrealistic at all. May I see the rest of the pages?'

'Robert, I was so taken aback, I didn't know what to say. I tried to think calmly and quickly, so I told Tom that we were trying to preserve the condition of the book and didn't want it handled very much. But I said perhaps a look at the first couple of pages would be alright. Oh, Robert, I was scared about letting the cat out of the bag.'

'Tom seemed happy enough with that, though, and he carefully looked at the first sketch and then the second.'

'Well,' he said, 'if you are right, then I reckon you have a valuable piece of art there.' And, to my utter relief, handed the sketchbook back to me.

'I thanked Tom profusely, and Stuart too, when we descended the stairs and arranged to meet up when Stuart was next in town. He rang for a taxicab for me, and I caught the tube at Tooting Broadway to here.'

'The sketchbook's safe?' asked Robert.

'It is. It's here in my bag.'

'So, it's as we hoped. A Turner sketchbook like no other.' Robert sounded like a proud and possessive father.

'Yes. We must decide what we are going to do with it.'

'No, there's no discussion to be had. I've told you before, I'm keeping it.'

'But Robert ...'

'No. It's mine, and no one is going to take it away from me. Not even you.' Robert spat the last three words out.

'But ...'

'No! And that's an end to it. Pass it to me. Now. Please.'

With much sadness at the vehemence of Robert's words, Jonathan extracted the book and handed it over.

'Thank you.'

Robert clutched the cloth-bound sketchbook, its worn cover enticing him with its secrets untold. Inside lay the lure of Byron's lustful indiscretions, a scandal waiting to erupt, captured in Turner's masterful pencil strokes. Ever since they had found it in that bookstore in Venice, Robert's equilibrium had undergone a considerable shift. Common sense had given way to passion, possibly to obsession. He hadn't noticed the change in how he now viewed the world. Until this point, he had been passive, agreeable, considerate. Had he paid attention to his psyche he would have seen instead an aggression, a fierceness that overrode all sound sensibilities. These changes had only happened as a consequence of being owned by the sketchbook.

Jonathan watched him with concern. 'Robert,' he almost whispered, 'I understand the historical value, but Lord Byron's private life, especially depicted in such…compromising situations… don't you think the world deserves to see this?'

Robert held the sketchbook tighter. 'Deserves? This isn't some grand historical document, Jonathan. It's … personal. No, this stays here, with me.'

'But think of what it reveals about Byron, about Romanticism itself! Imagine the impact – the discussions, the exhibitions…' Jonathan's voice rose, then faltered under Robert's glare. He sighed, his own gaze flitting between the sketchbook and Robert's impassioned face. He knew Robert's stubborn streak – as wide as the Thames – but now with a venom he hadn't shown before. It frightened Jonathan.

Robert's grip tightened on the book. The thought of strangers' eyes scrutinising these intimate sketches, dissecting Byron's private moments, repulsed him.

'No,' he said, his voice firm. 'It's not that simple, Jon.

Robert moved around to be close to Jonathan. He placed the sketchbook on the table, his eyes clamped on it. The worn cover seemed to crackle with unspoken desires, and he envisioned Byron's fiery spirit, forever tarnished by prurient curiosity.

'This is not for the public eye,' Robert continued. 'This sketchbook is a window into a world that shouldn't be exposed, not for public scrutiny.' He looked at Jonathan, his gaze softening. 'Don't you understand? It's not about Byron. It's about protecting something...fragile.'

Jonathan slumped back, a wave of disillusionment washing over him. He understood Robert's attachment, the allure of possessing a piece of history. But the potential for knowledge, for a deeper understanding of a literary giant, felt like a missed opportunity.

'But Robert,' he tried again, his voice laced with urgency, 'what if it gets into the wrong hands? Imagine it falling prey to some unscrupulous trader who exploited it for personal gain!'

Robert's face softened. He knew Jonathan's concern was genuine. 'It's not that simple, Jon,' he sighed, running a hand through his partner's hair. 'These are private moments, captured without consent. Sharing them feels wrong, somehow. You surely can understand that?'

He picked a loose piece of cotton from Jonathan's sweater. Silence descended. Robert stole a glance at Jonathan; his partner's usually gentle face etched with disappointment.

'Look,' Robert continued, his voice softer now, 'I understand your point. But can't it just be ours, Jon? A shared secret between us, a reminder of the hidden layers beneath the surface of both history and truth?'

He reached out, his hand hovering over Jonathan's. A plea for understanding. Jonathan met his gaze; his own eyes filled with a mixture of longing and acceptance. He nodded slowly. 'Alright, Robert, though I know you will always think of it as yours, not ours.'

He squeezed Jonathan's hand. A silent thank you.

Chapter Three

Andrea Rossi had, at last, completed his calculations and was satisfied that he was indeed a descendant of one Margherita Cogni. The family had long inferred that their lineage included this woman, but now he had proved the link.

He exhaled the MS cigarette smoke into the fug already circulating in his office and smiled in the fulfilment of his task, flicking closed his gold and lacquered Dunhill lighter and closed the new Verona marbled cigarette box on his desk.

There was nothing special about the family connections: no royal blood, no aristocratic members. But there were infamy and intrigue. And that was all down to his great-great-great grandmother.

His father had provided only a little information about the Cogni line, but nowhere near as much as his mother, Giulia, could have done had she not contracted tuberculosis and died when he was eight. He knew his maternal grandfather, Alessandro, however, and knew from him directly that Alessandro had been born in

Venice in 1881. At the age of eighteen, Andrea had heard of the old man's death in that city. There was a funeral, of course, but neither he nor his father bothered to attend.

He had quite liked his grandfather and had enjoyed the stories told to him when they saw each other either in Venice or at home in Milan when the old man visited. Some of the stories sounded a little far-fetched even to his young ears, but he had regaled him with tales of a famous Lord Byron and their relative, Margherita Cogni.

One such story concerned Margherita meeting an English artist, thought to be JMW Turner, in Lord Byron's house and being given a sketchbook by him, in which it was believed she had been sketched alongside Byron himself. It was further said that she was enamoured with Turner and that he gave her the sketchbook as a token of his admiration of her when he departed the palazzo.

Rossi had been sure that Margherita would have treasured the book and kept it with her, safe, passing it on to future generations as a valued heirloom. When he had questioned his grandfather about it two years before his death, Alessandro had said that he understood the sketchbook was real but didn't know what had happened to it. He had pushed the old man hard to recall its existence, but when he couldn't, Andrea grew petulant and continued to harass the man into providing an answer, growing angry when he couldn't or wouldn't.

Finally, today, Andrea had received the last piece of information from the Civil Status Office in Venice to complete the genealogical jigsaw: the certificate of birth of Francesco Cogni, son of Paulo and Margherita Cogni. The line was now complete. His forebear really had not simply been a character in his grandfather's stories. She really had existed and had lived with Byron in the Palazzo Mocenigo in Venice, as his grandfather had said.

It was a trait of Andrea Rossi's to constantly seek opportunities to improve his personal wealth and status as a businessman and entrepreneur. His ability to acquire ailing businesses cheaply and turn them around before selling them at vastly inflated prices was the key to his fortune and was legendary in Milan. As was his ruthlessness in achieving his own ends and his apparent disregard for the feelings or needs of those he chose to 'help' free themselves from their struggling operations.

His sponsorship and board membership of the chamber orchestra Angelicum Orchestra of Milan did, however, reflect a pleasanter aspect of his character, and there could be no doubt that he had good taste. His contemporaries saw his single-minded pursuit of perfection as either positive or negative, depending on whether one shared his ideals.

Still holding the birth certificate, Rossi began to wonder what had happened to that sketchbook. *I have to find out where it is, if it still exists. It is possibly worth a lot of money, and besides, as an heir, I am entitled to it. I shall have it.*

He took another considered drag on his cigarette. It occurred to him that the best place to start was the pensione in Venice, which the family had operated until the war in 1939. He was a wealthy enough businessman to afford to take time away, so he found the telephone number for the Gritti in Venice and booked himself a room for the following two nights. Then, he organised a seat on the train, leaving Milan for Venice the next morning.

After checking into his hotel room and unpacking, he returned to the hotel lobby and asked the concierge to have a water taxi sent to take him to the location in San Polo, which he remembered from visiting his grandfather when he was younger. The taxi came promptly; the pilot collecting him from the lobby and escorting Andrea to the launch, where he gave the pilot an address on the Rio di San Polo. He despatched his fare quickly at that location, for which he received a modest tip.

Rossi walked along the partially remembered calles and alleys until he reached the spot where his family's pensione had stood. He had almost walked past it; it had changed so much, but this was the place. The façade was freshly rendered in cream with emerald green shutters at its eight windows and a front door of the same colour. It had a modern elegance that he didn't remember of the crumbling building. He pushed open the door and entered a sleek-looking reception area with a teak-coloured desk and flooring set off by bright walls of a pale cream and modern gilt surround mirrors reflecting soft lamps and down lights. Money had clearly been spent here.

'Good morning, sir. How may I help you?' A smiling, pleasant-looking woman of about thirty-eight asked in what Rossi discerned as a Neapolitan accent, certainly not Venetian, from over the reception desk.

'I should like to speak with the owner, if I may,' Rossi said in his distinct Lombard accent.

The woman's smile slipped into a serious concern. 'Is anything the matter? May I help?'

'Are you the owner?' The emphasis falling on the word 'you'. Andrea disliked being questioned about what he wanted. He expected others to leap to satisfy his demands.

'My husband and I run this pensione. Is something wrong?'

'I apologise,' he lied. 'My family used to own this business, and I am looking for information about it.'

'I see. What is your name?'

'Rossi. Andrea Rossi, but my family's name is Cogni.'

Isabella Canda had heard that name when she and her Venetian husband, Giorgio, first bought the pensione three years ago.

'I am familiar with the name. What do you wish to know, and I will try to help you?'

'Thank you, Signora ...?'

'Canda.'

'Signora Canda, when you purchased this business, did you find anything that may have belonged to my family?'

'I seem to recall that the pensione was empty and very dirty when we took it over. We had to clean every room on every floor before we could begin the modernisation that we had planned to make the place more,' Isabella hesitated, 'respectable.'

She paused.

'And?' Irritation crept into Rossi's tone.

'Well, possibly. In the attic room, my husband found a few rags and other things in a box. We wanted to get things cleaned up, so we were about to throw the stuff out when we saw a tatty-looking book. Giorgio, my husband, had a quick glance at it and told me it had some drawings in it. He is a practical man and not very interested in art, so I told him not to discard it, as someone may find it interesting. I would take it to a bookstore in a day or two.'

'And did you?'

'Eventually, yes.'

'When?' He snapped.

'We were very busy getting the pensione updated and presentable, you understand.'

'When?' He demanded.

Isabella found his manner distasteful. 'Last year sometime. We were very busy, as I say and ...'

'Which store?'

There was no pleasantness in Rossi's voice now, and Isabella wanted him gone.

'An old bookstore in Santa Croce, in a piazza close to Rio Marin. I don't recall its name.' She could if she put her mind to it, but she didn't think he was worth the effort.

'Was anything else left?'

'No.' she replied, maintaining her sense of professionalism.

'How do I get to the piazza?'

Isabella produced a map of Venice and pointed to where the piazza was, as far as she could recall. Rossi took the map and left. There were no thanks or farewells.

'What an unpleasant person!'

Even though Santa Croce was the smallest of Venice's districts, Andrea Rossi realised that, without an address, he wouldn't know where to start. So, he found a café close to Ponte San Polo, ordered a coffee and considered how he would find the bookstore. He realised it was pointless to set off on foot, hoping to find the bookstore in Santa Croce. That 'bitch' in the pensione had been less than helpful in assisting him to locate it, so it was probably best, he concluded, to return to his hotel to see if they could point him in the right direction.

He finished his coffee, which he found sub-standard, and picked up a taxi. He was back at his hotel within minutes. Rossi sought the services of the hotel's concierge, but he was unable to provide Rossi with an address but vowed to find out and provide an answer as soon as possible. To Rossi, that meant within about twenty minutes. To the concierge, with his other duties, that meant what he had said; as soon as possible.

Rossi waited impatiently in his room. He tried reading but couldn't settle down to the newspaper. He tried listening to the radio but found the music irritable. An hour passed like this, and still he waited, getting more frustrated by the minute. Then, at last, the telephone rang. He wrote the address the concierge gave him on the hotel notepad and, with a gruff 'thank you,' hung up.

Checking his watch, Rossi saw it was still siesta. He was hungry, so he ordered some food in his room and waited until it was a suitable time to go to Campo San Giacomo da l'Orio. Now that he had the address, his surliness softened, and he was able to enjoy his lunch.

At two-thirty, Rossi gave the taxi pilot the instruction to take him to Ponte Ruga Bella, and at three o'clock exactly, he had alighted at the steps next to the bridge and was walking past the Chiesa Parrocchiale on his left, heading into the irregular-shaped, tree stippled campo. Near the far end of the campo, there was a bookstore. He had found it, and soon the sketchbook would be his.

He strode over to it, underneath the large luxuriant tree offering shade and coolness ignored by Rossi, and back into the sun and the crumbling buildings to his right. The bookstore's double green doors were folded back, displaying an entrance like an open mouth, dark inside, calling him in. Unlike the others sitting around in the shade, talking and looking relaxed, he was now tense with anticipation as he strode to the store.

When Guido Zampelli told Rossi that the sketchbook had indeed come into his possession but that he had sold it, Rossi was apoplectic.

'The book is mine. I own it. You had no right to sell it.' His voice quivered with rage.

Guido was taken aback. 'Now, wait a moment ...'

'No, I will not wait. How dare you!'

'I think you had better calm down so we can discuss this quietly. Shouting will get you nowhere.'

'Don't tell me what to do.' Rossi continued his barrage, throwing his arms around. Guido was finding it hard to follow Rossi's accent and gestures.

The two other customers in the store eased their way past the two men and slunk out into the campo.

Guido was familiar with irate and difficult customers from his days as a sommelier, so knew how to manage a situation like this. 'What is it you want me to do, Mr ...?'

'Never mind who I am. I want my sketchbook.'

'My name is Guido Zampelli. I own this bookstore. Won't you let me know who I am talking with?' He spoke quietly and slowly, taking the aggression out of the situation.

'Rossi. The name's Rossi.'

'Thank you, Mr Rossi. If I remember correctly, the sketchbook came to me from a woman several weeks ago. Would that be right?'

'Yes.'

'Was she a relative of yours?'

'No, she was the owner of a pensione that my family had connections with.'

'Here in Venice?'

'Yes.'

The conversation was now more controlled; the vitriol having gone from Rossi as he realised there would be no point in continuing his animosity.

'I'm very sorry, Mr Rossi, I had no idea that the book didn't belong to her, but, as I say, it has been sold.'

'To whom do you know?'

'Yes, to an Englishman who was on holiday in Venice a little while ago.'

'Do you know his name?'

'I do, yes. I have his details, as he wanted me to locate and send him some books. Wait, I'll get the information.'

Hope returned to Rossi as he waited for Zampelli's return.

'I have written down his details for you. Here,' Guido handed over a sheet of paper with Robert Ferngrove's information on it.

'Thank you, Mr Zampelli. I apologise for my behaviour earlier, but I am most eager to regain my property. Would you be so kind as to telephone for a taxi to pick me up at Ponte Ruga Bella?'

Back in his hotel room, Rossi began making plans. He determined that the immediate course of action when he was back home in Milan was to telephone the London number and speak to this Robert Ferngrove, explain who he was and insist – no, that was too demonstrative – request that the sketchbook be returned to his family. He was sure this person would understand when the circumstances were explained to him.'

Andrea Rossi disliked using the telephone at the best of times, but when it involved operators, it increased his angst no end. Now, he had to utilise the services of an international operator to book his call. This was going to cost a lot of lira.

An hour after booking the call, Rossi's telephone rang. The operator told him she was connecting to the number through the London switchboard. There were several squeaks and pops, then the sound of ringing.

'Hello, Ferngrove and Spencer's', the somewhat effeminate male voice announced.

'Hello, my name is Rossi, Andrea Rossi. I am calling from Milan in Italy.' He said in excellent English. 'I wish to speak to Robert Ferngrove.'

'I am sorry, but he is not in the shop this afternoon. May I help you? I am his partner, Jonathan Spencer.'

'No. It is with him that I must speak. Will he be available tomorrow?'

'Yes. Are you sure I cannot assist?'

'Cazzo! Sorry. No. I will try to call again tomorrow.'

The next day, the international operator announced that line issues were causing lengthy delays in calls to England, and, no, she couldn't say how long it would be before he could make his call. Perhaps tomorrow.

This is stupido, he thought as he hung up the telephone. It then occurred to him to write to one of his business associates in London to ask her to visit Ferngrove's bookshop and get an impression of what he and his partner were like. Then, he would have an idea of who he would be dealing with.

I must speak to his face, not on the telephone, anyway, he decided. So, would wait as patiently as he could until he received the reply from Sarah Mulholland.

When her letter reached him several days later, Miss Mulholand gave him a good account of what she thought of Mr Ferngrove and his partner – not much – and described the shop and its location.

He picked up the telephone and dialled the operator. 'Buongiorno, per favore, portami Alitalia.' He would fly to London and meet with Robert Ferngrove.

There was no doubt in Rossi's mind that this was all worthwhile. The sketchbook belonged to him. He was going to London to get it.

Chapter Four

The shop bell tinged, and Joanna looked up to see a man entering. She took in a tall, fit, black-haired man in an expensive-looking, stylish grey suit, white shirt, and conservatively patterned tie. Against the door frame, she perceived his height to be about six feet, perhaps a fraction over. She saw a very attractive man a little older than she was, but not much. The sight pleased her.

She stood and glided out of the kitchen area at the rear of the shop, happily keeping her eyes on the customer. She wasn't conscious of her dilated pupils nor of her heart beating a little faster than normal as she passed some of the book displays toward him.

He was glancing at the books as he sauntered around them, heading for the till area. Not a lot of space existed between the small maze of various book displays and bookshelves, but Joanna timed her approach to the till area just as the good-looking man reached it.

'Good morning,' she said, her voice bordering on obsequiousness and pleasure while her nose registered the spicy aromatics of an expensive aftershave, 'may I be of assistance?' Being a shop assistant gave her the perfect opportunity to approach people without the embarrassment of coyness that she would have otherwise suffered had the situation occurred elsewhere.

'Good morning to you, also.' He smiled. She looked delightful, he thought.

English spoken with what seemed to her an Italian accent brought her further excitement.

'I wish to speak with Mr Ferngrove if you please?'

'I'm very sorry but both Mr Ferngrove and Mr Spencer are away in Yorkshire on a book buying trip. They left yesterday, and I don't expect them back for possibly a week. Is there something I can help you with? I am Mr Ferngrove's sister, Joanna.' She said wittingly.

'Perhaps.' The voice not completely hiding the feeling of annoyance. 'Yes, perhaps. I am an acquaintance of Mr Ferngrove and have learned from a bookstore owner in Italy that we have a mutual interest in certain items. I am here to discuss this with him but am most happy to wait until he has returned.' He smiled at Joanna. She, charmed by the smile, gave a warm smile back. Her stomach tightened, either as a sexual response or from trepidation.

He sensed that, like so many other women, Robert Ferngrove's sister found him interesting. That was fine by him. He also found her attractive. She had a lovely body, a pretty face, and a soft voice that he found most appealing. If he had to wait until Ferngrove returned, then at least he could enjoy her company.

'As I am to wait for his return, would you do me the honour of assisting me? I would enjoy you telling me about London, this shop,' he gesticulated around it, 'and, of course, about you.' Did she really blush?

'Do you not live in London?' She asked.

'No, I am from Italy, so your company would be most welcome. Would you have a dinner with me? I think that would be most enjoyable.'

Joanna knew she should take time to think this over. Her upbringing deemed it so. After all, she knew nothing about this man, didn't even know his name. So, it came as a shock even to her when she said, 'Yes, I'd like that.' She attempted to convince herself that it was so she could eat a decent meal for once. It crossed her mind, but she didn't believe it.

'Would this evening be acceptable to you, Joanna?'

Oh, he remembers my name, she thought. 'Yes, that would be fine.'

'I do not know the names of reputable restaurants in London. Would you be happy to dine at my hotel's restaurant?'

With some hesitation now, Joanna answered. 'But, of course. Thank you.'

'Good, I shall book a table for seven-thirty. Are you able to get to the Savoy by that time?'

'Oh, I'll manage it.' She felt easier now.

'Excellent. Until then.'

He took her hand and bowed slightly. She thought he was actually going to kiss it, but he just turned to leave.

'I don't know your name. Who should I ask for at the hotel?'

'I shall be waiting in the lobby for you. But the name is Rossi. Andrea Rossi. Don't be late.'

The taxi pulled up outside the entrance to the hotel. This manner of transport was an extravagance she could little afford but one that had to be met. There was no other way she could have travelled in her best 'little black dress'. It was going to be worth it.

She paid the driver while one of the liveried doormen opened the taxi's passenger door and helped her step out and into the entrance with its revolving doors leading to the black and white chequered floor of the lobby. True to his word, Andrea Rossi was standing directly ahead at the top of the stairs leading down to the lounge, talking to a blonde woman of indeterminate age and wealth.

As Joanna approached the couple, she saw Andrea place a hand on the woman's arm, at which point she left him, and he turned to face Joanna, moving towards him. He thought she looked stunningly attractive and walked with grace and confidence.

'Perfect timing,' he said. 'Thank you. I detest people not having the courtesy to arrive at a scheduled time.'

'My pleasure, I can assure you.' Joanna purred.

'Let us have a drink before going through for dinner.' It was a statement rather than a request from Andrea, to which Joanna was more than happy to agree. The Beaumont was busy and smoky. They found a table. Joanna loved the opulence and glamour of the bar.

Andrea ordered a glass of champagne for each of them, and he lit a cigarette. 'I do not offer a cigarette to you Joanna as I do not like to see a woman smoking.'

'That is quite alright, Andrea, thank you. I don't smoke.'

They chatted as best they could over the clammer of voices around them about things in general – the weather, of course, both in London and in Milan and other innocuous pleasantries. After a few moments, a staff member approached Rossi to advise that his table in the Grill awaited him whenever he would care to go through.

Andrea and Joanna finished their drinks and were escorted to their table by the patiently waiting staff member.

The meal and the wine were exquisite. They were able to talk more intimately in the restaurant and each of them learned a lot about the other. Andrea Rossi was unmarried and lived in an apartment in Milan; he was a successful entrepreneur involved with business acquisitions and development – whatever that meant, Joanna didn't know – throughout Europe. He had a love of fine things and was passionate about music. Joanna smiled and said that she shared a similar love and went on to explain about her being an unemployed cellist.

'I fully understand. It must be so hard for women musicians.'

Joanna couldn't believe a man would have such sympathies for her and other women's plight in getting work in an orchestra. 'Yes, it is. It seems we are doomed to roles of teaching only.'

'But tell me,' Andrea continued, diverting the conversation, 'where do you fit in with the bookshop in Cecil Court? Are you a part owner?'

'No, the shop belongs to my brother and his partner. I help out occasionally, like now, when they go away.'

'They are very lucky to have you do this for them.'

'No, not at all.' She could feel herself reddening again – must be the wine. 'I enjoy it, and I get paid a little for it. In fact, I have to be there tomorrow to open up,' she said, looking alarmedly at her watch and seeing the time. 'Oh lord, it's getting late. I hadn't realised. I really should be going.'

'Must you? You could stay here tonight.'

The invitation took Joanna by complete surprise. She would love to, wanted to. He was a gorgeous man. She was on the point of agreeing, but then something indefinable told her, No, not yet.

'Thank you, Andrea. It's been a wonderful evening, and I have truly enjoyed your company, but I'll make my way home.'

Normally, Andrea would have resented such a rejection, but strangely, he admired her propriety.

'It has been a pleasure to share this evening with you, Joanna. Thank you.'

'I will just powder my nose before I leave.' And she rose and headed for the ladies' restroom.

Andrea had the meal and drinks charged to his room, and when Joanna returned, they went together to the lobby, where the concierge organised a taxi for Joanna. He kissed her cheek prior to her settling into her seat in the rear of the cab, and as the taxi pulled away, she smiled at the enjoyment that she had experienced because of Andrea.

The flowers that she signed for the next morning at the shop were astonishing. Twelve long-stem red roses. The card read, 'Per una bella signorina'. Joanna's forced, calm demeanour betrayed her inner frenzy. 'Oh, my!' Her broad smile lit up the already bright shop.

It has only been one evening. Don't get carried away, you stupid woman. But he was so thoughtful and caring. Loving? Maybe. You don't know anything about him.

The customer standing in front of her feigning patience said she was looking for an eighteenth-century map of London. Did she have one? Joanna, coming to her senses, apologised for not being able to help and pointed her in the direction of a shop further down the Court that could probably assist.

'Lovely flowers,' the customer said as she left the shop.

Joanna went to the back area in search of something in which to put them, but the best she could do was leave them laying in the tiny sink in a small amount of water to keep them fresh.

The ringing telephone startled her. 'Ferngrove and Spencer. How can I help you?'

'Morning, Jo.'

'Robbie, how are you?'

'Very well, thanks. We're off to the auction at Stanbury House shortly, so thought I'd call and see if all was well at your end.'

'Yes, all is very well here. You had an Italian man asking for you in the shop yesterday.'

'What, actually there in person?'

'Yes.'

'Did he give you his name? It wasn't Guido Zampelli, by any chance?'

'No, it was Andrea Rossi. He said he was an acquaintance of both yours and a bookshop owner in Italy.'

'Damn, he must be an associate of Guido's. Did he say what he wanted?'

'He needs to talk to you about some books and that he will return when you are back. He is a deliciously attractive man, Robbie. My type, not yours,' she teased. 'In fact, he took me to dinner last night.' She said this with an upward inflexion in her voice.

'Oh, did he?'

'Mmm,' she purred. 'to the Savoy. And he had roses delivered to me at the shop just now.'

'Lucky you.'

'Yes, I'm sure you'll like him when you meet. He's staying in London. No need to hurry back.'

'I get the picture. Well, have fun. Be careful. I'll call you again in a couple of days. Bye.'

'Bye.'

Robert looked forward to meeting up with Mr Rossi. Guido, in Venice, he thought, seemed to be keeping his word about business dealings. That would be excellent. But for now, onto Stanbury House.

It was 4.45 pm when Andrea came into the shop. She knew it was unprofessional of her, but she hurried the customer through his purchase and out of the door before turning, smiling, to greet him.

'Hello,' she said. 'The flowers were absolutely lovely. They came this morning. Thank you so much, Andrea. They need some fresh water and a suitable vase, though, now.'

'It is my pleasure. I had an enjoyable evening. Say, why don't we get a taxi and take your flowers to your home? You can look after them, and then we will go out somewhere.'

'What, all the way to Crouch End at this time of day?'

'Certainly. You must look after the flowers.'

And so, closing the shop at 5 pm, they walked to Charing Cross Road and hailed a taxi to take them to Joanna's ground-floor flat. Lucy, her flatmate, was not at home when they reached it, and, thankfully, she realised their usual mess was minimal.

The note from Lucy on the dining table announced that she 'Won't be home tonight – staying with Susie. xx' I wonder what those two are up to, Joanna pondered.

Then, a thought came to her, she turned around to Andrea and asked, 'Why don't we stay here tonight? I can cook you a pretty awful meal, and we have a wine that was once reputably related to a grape. What do you think?'

'If it is not too much trouble, I am prepared to risk it!'

'Right, well, you just sit over there, and I'll quickly get changed. I can't believe I'm doing this after that splendid meal last night. Please forgive me,' she said with a smile.

But Andrea didn't want to sit. 'Do you mind if I look at your records?'

'No, not at all. Put something on if you like. I'm sure you'll find the player easy to operate,' she said as she disappeared into a hallway and then her bedroom.

The charm and sunshine of Boccherini's Cello Concerto in G rose from the speakers. 'Oh, Andrea, what a choice,' Joanna called from her room. 'I had to perform that for my final exams,' she continued as she came back into the living room.

'It is one of my favourite cello pieces. I am surprised to see you have the record and am even more surprised to know that you can play it. Perhaps, instead of the record, you could play the solo part?'

'What now? What about dinner?'

'The dinner can wait. I would love to hear you play. It is one of my favourites and one that the Milan Chamber Orchestra plays quite well.'

'You know the Milan Chamber Orchestra?'

'Yes. Now, if it is here, go and get your cello.' He turned off the record player.

Joanna went back to her bedroom and returned carrying her well-travelled cello case. She propped this up against the dining table, went back for her stool, and placed it facing Andrea. From the case, she brought out her pride and joy – the Pierre Marcel that her parents had bought for her after graduating. With the cello prepared, Joanna sat with her legs apart and the instrument comfortably positioned in between. Andrea looked impressed. She played beautifully and better than he had imagined.

'My goodness, Joanna, that was excellent. How would you like to play it in the orchestra?'

'Which orchestra?' Joanna asked with excitement.

'Milan, of course.'

'But how? I mean, how can that be possible?'

'Well, I told you I knew the Milan Chamber Orchestra; I am, in fact, on their board and can arrange for an audition for you, which I know you will pass.'

'I don't understand, Andrea. Do you mean go to Italy?'

'Yes, that would be necessary.'

'But I can't. Can I? I can't just leave everything here.' But Joanna didn't truly think that to be the case, and her voice supported that belief. *Could I really do this?*

Honestly? She asked herself rather than Andrea. *Yes, I can, can't I? Why not?* She responded to herself.

'Oh, Andrea!'

Chapter Five

There was so much to think about; Joanna barely slept that night. After an exciting, mediocre dinner, during which Andrea and she talked a lot about the reality of what he was going to do for her, sleep was the last thing her mind wanted. Her body disputed this, however.

What an incredible evening, she found herself repeating again and again. *I'm going to Milan.* And then, the doubts. *How do I know this is for real You don't know this man, but you're going to trust him to take you to Italy. No, trust your feelings, Joanna. It feels right – doesn't it? – it does. If it doesn't work out, you can always come home. You don't even know the language. Where will you live? Oh, stop it. Just ask yourself one simple question: Do you want to do it? Yes!*

She rose on Sunday morning, a wreck but stimulated by the prospect before her. Her brain told her she ought to make a plan of what she had to do to make this come about. Not being the most methodical of people, this was her first hurdle. A wash, a coffee, a notepad, and pen.

'Timing,' Joanna wrote, and next to it, '1. When can Andrea organise the audition? 2. After giving notice on the flat to Lucy.' *Oh, poor Lucy, I hope she'll be all right and can find another flatmate.*

And so, she went on, listing all the things she could think of to be ticked off as they were done.

She sipped another cup of coffee and thought of Andrea again. He hadn't pursued the possibility of staying the night, sensing that Joanna's excitement about the audition would occupy her mind and had left to find a taxi at the Clock Tower nearby, but not before she allowed him to embrace and kiss her. He said he would telephone her later on Sunday, but Joanna had to say that there was no telephone in the flat. 'Then, I shall have to wait until Monday morning and ring you at the shop.' Disappointedly, Joanna had to accept the arrangement.

When Lucy returned home later that morning, she found Joanna still in her dressing gown, writing away at the dining table.

'A bit slobby, aren't we?' she said mockingly.

'Hello, Luce. How was Susie?'

'Not bad. I'll tell you more in a minute. I just want to dump my things and get a coffee. What's all the writing? You turning novelist or something?'

'I'll have another one,' called Joanna. 'No, nothing like that. I'm making a list.'

Lucy came in with the coffees and sat at the table with Joanna.

'Susie's rather down. Her landlord's given her notice to quit her flat, and the thought of looking around for another flat as nice as that is depressing for her.'

'That's sad, but I have an idea that might cheer her up. She could move in here.'

'What? How? There isn't room.'

'There may be soon.' Joanna went on to explain about the potential move to Italy.

'Oh no. I shall be so sorry to see you go, but what an opportunity for you. I know we've talked about setting up our ensemble, but this would be brilliant for you. It is kosher, isn't it?'

'I think so,' and she went on to tell Lucy about Andrea.

'Well, you're a dark horse, I must say. How long have you known him?'

Joanna thought for a moment. 'Oh, goodness. Two days. Just two days, it seems like for ages.'

'Good for you, girl. I'm really happy for you. And, yes, I'm sure Susie will be thrilled to come here. It will be cheaper for her too, sharing. I'll miss you, though. I'll come for a holiday!'

'Steady on, I'm not there yet.'

'Good morning, Joanna.'

'Andrea! Good morning to you, too. Did you have an enjoyable day yesterday?'

'No, not especially. I wanted to be with you but spent my time with someone I met on Friday.'

Joanna immediately pictured the blonde woman at the hotel and felt a slight pang of jealousy.

'Will you be coming into the shop?'

'Not until five o'clock, again, if that's all right. We could go for a drink and a talk.'

'That's fine. I'll look forward to it.'

'Ciao, then Joanna.'

She couldn't believe she said 'Ciao' back to him.

At almost eleven, Robert rang.

'We've had a most successful trip, Jo, and bought a rather large number of books, which we're having delivered to the shop. There are far too many to bring back on the train. Jonathan's organising that as we speak.'

'That's wonderful, Robbie. I'm so glad it was a worthwhile trip.'

'So, we will be home again on Wednesday. We're going to have a celebratory dinner up here tonight, and one of the locals has offered to show us around a bit tomorrow. We'll catch the early morning train to Kings

Cross the next day and should be at the shop around noon. Everything all right with you?'

'Yes. There's lots to tell you, and, of course, you will get to meet Andrea. I mean Mr Rossi, probably on Wednesday, if that's acceptable?'

'I'm looking forward to it. There could be some good business to be had through him. Have you made any decent sales?'

The discussion continued in a business-like fashion for a little longer before Robert rang off, leaving Joanna in excited anticipation for five o'clock.

The Bear and Staff public house on Bear Street was just a short stroll from the shop. Andrea had said he wanted to visit a good London pub, as he heard about them many times in Italy. Joanna had passed this one when out and about and thought he would enjoy it. Being a Monday, the bar wasn't very busy, and they easily found a table to which Andrea brought his pint of bitter and Joanna's gin and tonic.

'I hadn't considered you a beer man,' she grinned.

'I am not, but I have to try it. Be the real Englishman,' he joked. He took a sip, and it was evident from his facial expression that it wasn't quite as he had expected.

'Now, Joanna, I have today sent a telegraph to the personnel manager of the orchestra – he is the man who organises auditions – asking him for dates when you may attend. I expect to hear tomorrow, but I think it will be soon.'

She took a good quantity of her drink before exclaimed, 'Andrea. Thank you so much for this. I can't believe you are doing this for me. It seems quite surreal.'

'No, don't thank me, Joanna. You have an exceptional talent which the orchestra will benefit from, and you deserve to be rewarded for your art. And besides, I do it for me, too. I like you very much and want to make us both happy.'

Joanna was still amazed that this wonderful man, whom she had known for but a few days, felt this way about her and was doing all this for her.

'When I receive the dates for the audition, you will choose which is good for you, and I will arrange for us to go. You have a passport, yes? Good, so tomorrow, we will plan the journey more.'

Joanna was shaking her head in almost disbelief. 'I cannot believe it. I just can't.'

'Please accept it is happening and do not disbelieve. Be happy. Enjoy. Now, I must buy a whisky and not have this beer. I think I make a better Scottish man than English,' he laughed.

On his return to the table with his whisky and another gin and tonic, Joanna announced that her brother, Robert, and his partner, Jonathan, would be in the shop in two days' time and, if it were convenient, she would telephone Andrea at his hotel so that he could then come to the shop and meet them. Andrea said that he would appreciate the call and would come straight away.

'I am very much looking forward to meeting your brother.'

This, too, pleased Joanna. How wonderful everything was turning out.

'Please, tell me what he is like.'

'Well, he's awfully sweet and caring. He and I get on famously. He is not manly in the sort of way you are but has a wonderful temperament. I am sure you two will get on well. He isn't tall. And he likes to dress well. And, of course, he loves his books. You will find out for yourself in a couple of days. Now, tell me what is going to happen when we choose a date for the audition.'

So, Andrea explained that, because of the size of the cello and other baggage, it would be necessary to go by train and boat, not by air. 'The journey will be long, I am sorry to say. I will work out an itinerary that I think will include a boat train from here to Paris and then another train to Milan. You will stay in a nice hotel close to my apartment, and I can spend a little time showing you my city. Will that be acceptable to you? Then, when you have the position ...'

'Andrea, you mean "if" I get the position.'

'I mean what I say. I have a great influence on the orchestra. You will get the position. So, when you have it, you will come to Milan, and I will find you a good place to stay and show you how you can live in the city. But that is later when the season commences. I regret that this year's programme has begun, so you will only be able to participate in their off-season activities.'

'It all sounds so wonderful and simple. Thank you, Andrea.'

'Come, finish your drink. It is still early. Perhaps we could go to the theatre or a concert?'

Andrea rang Joanna at the shop the next day to tell her that the orchestra's personnel manager had offered four dates for an audition. She wrote them down on a notepad. They were all quite soon, and she had no preference.

'Perhaps we take the second date,' suggested Andrea. 'That way, we have time to get to Milan without rushing, but it is not too far in the future. Yes? And I need to get back and do some work.'

'I agree. So, Thursday, the twenty-eighth of September it is then.'

The rest of the day passed routinely for Joanna in the shop, although she spent some time mulling over what clothes to take with her and trying to find information about Milan and its chamber orchestra from the shop's books but found them limited.

Just after noon the next day, Robert and Jonathan came bumping their way through the shop doorway, bags in hand and looking every bit the weary rail travellers, they were.

'Gosh, Robbie, Jonathan, you look bushed.'

They dumped their bags at the back of the shop and greeted and kissed each other in welcome.

'Come and sit down. I'll make a nice cup of tea.'

'That would be lovely, thank you, Joanna. Robert, do you want to show Joanna what we brought her back?'

Robert opened his case. The musical score lay flat on top of his clothes. He removed it and handed it to Joanna.

'I remember you saying you had to learn this inside out and that you really liked it, so when we saw it, amongst other scores at one of the auctions, we thought it would be perfect for you. I know you have this already, but this is a signed one.'

Joanna took the score from him and looked astounded as she saw the date May 23, 1911, and the signature of Pablo Casals on the Boccherini Concerto score.

'My God, Robbie, this is fantastic and so propitious. I'll explain in a mo'. You know Casals is my absolute idol. Oh God, thank you, darling. Thank you. Look,' she enthused, opening the score, 'here are his markings. Amazing.'

'I think we can say that your sister is pleased with her gift.' Grinned Jonathan.

'It is truly uncanny, Jon, Robbie. It is because of this piece that I am going for an audition with the Orchestra dell'Angellicum di Milano.' She proudly stated.

'Where are they? Not ... Milan?'

'Oh, Robbie, you can be so dense sometimes,' she teased. 'Of course, Milan.'

'But how? What? When? Tell all, do!'

They sat themselves down on the stools at the back of the shop.

'I'll make the tea,' said Jonathan. 'You'd better get on with your tale, or I think you might burst.'

'Wait a moment, I have to make a phone call. It has relevance to all this.' Joanna called the number Andrea had given her, and the two boys overheard, 'Good afternoon, Savoy Hotel.' Two pairs of male eyebrows raised simultaneously. 'Hello, may I speak to Mr Rossi, Andrea Rossi? He is staying with you. This is Joanna Ferngrove.'

Within seconds, Joanna – and the two boys – were listening to the dulcet, Italian tones of Andrea Rossi.

'Joanna. How lovely to hear from you! Is it time for me to come to see your brother?'

'Yes, Andrea. Robert and Jonathan are back now, so you can come over whenever it is convenient.'

'It is convenient now. I will be happy to see you very soon.' He hung up abruptly.

'The Savoy! This Rossi fellow is staying at the Savoy?' Robert was incredulous. 'A representative of Guido Zampelli, a second-hand bookseller in Venice, staying there! Seems odd.'

Jonathan poured the tea, and the two boys paused, awaiting an explanation from Joanna.

'Well, I don't know where to begin,' she stammered, then presented the facts as she understood them. Yes, Mr Rossi was here to discuss a book arrangement with them. He is also a successful businessman. It is true, she had got to know him very well. He was charming. Certainly, she had had dinner with him at the Savoy – eyebrows were again raised. And yes, he had visited her at her flat, where she had played for him. Yes, it was Boccherini – now, they could understand the poignancy of their gift for her – and, yes, on the strength of that performance, he had offered her an audition at his Milan orchestra – eyebrows were lowered – to which she would be going on the twenty-third. Yes, she rather thought she had fallen for him. She further believed he had strong feelings for her, and no, they hadn't been to bed together.

Silence.

'Good God, girl. Have you had time to sell any books?'

She sipped her tea, feeling quite smug and content with life.

'Andrea is on his way over to us now. So, you will have what I have relayed to you confirmed. You'll like him. I know you will.'

They sipped their teas and waited in anticipatory silence.

The shop bell sounded 'ting'. They all looked towards the sound.

Chapter Six

The man who entered the shop wore a grey gaberdine mac and trilby hat. Robert looked at Joanna, who shook her head. Jonathan saw this and rose to assist the customer. With the shop door still open, another man entered. He was tall, dressed in a casual blue jacket with a red pocket handkerchief, an open-neck light blue shirt, and bone-coloured belted slacks. Robert thought he looked rather stylish. He looked again at Joanna, but she had already left her seat and was moving over to meet the man. Robert did likewise.

'Hello, Andrea.' Joanna moved to kiss his cheek, but Andrea turned to face the approaching Robert. She felt a little embarrassed.

Realising his rudeness, Andrea said, 'I apologise, Joanna,' and bent down to kiss her on both cheeks, then said, looking at Robert again, 'I am Rossi. Andrea Rossi. You are Joanna's brother?'

'Hello. Yes. I am Robert Ferngrove. And that man over there with the customer is my partner, Jonathan Spencer.

I am very pleased to meet you, Mr Rossi.' They shook hands.

'We have much to discuss, Mr Ferngrove, and I must leave for home soon. This,' Rossi gesticulated to the shop, 'is not a convenient place to talk. Perhaps you will come to my hotel.'

Robert had the impression Rossi was used to giving instructions, and he felt this was not merely a request but an expectation on his part.

'Yes, of course. When ...'

'Now would be acceptable to me.'

'But the shop. Erm, perhaps, Joanna, you would look after it while we are gone?'

'Sorry, Robbie, but I'm coming with you.'

Jonathan joined them. 'That chap didn't really know what he wanted but was going to look into some of the other shops in the Court. Hello.' He extended his hand to Rossi, who shook it perfunctorily, noticing only that it felt a little soft. 'I'm Jonathan Spencer.'

'Hello, Mr Spencer.'

'Jonathan, Mr Rossi wishes to talk about the arrangement at his hotel, but I don't think both of us will need to be there. Would you mind holding the fort here?'

Jonathan felt put out. 'What about Joanna? Couldn't she stay here?'

'No, she's coming with us.'

'Oh. I see. All right.'

'You could join us after the shop closes.' Robert said.

'Yes, I could do that, perhaps.'

'That's settled then,' said Robert, impervious to his partner's feelings. 'Is it the Savoy still, Mr Rossi?'

'That is correct. We shall sit in the lobby area. We will catch a taxi now. Come.'

'That's all right, isn't it, Jon?' Robert asked. 'We can collect our bags later this evening. I'll just take my satchel.'

Jonathan knew the satchel contained the sketchbook. *Doesn't he trust me with it?* he asked himself.

They left. Jonathan retreated to the rear of the shop, sulked, and studied Joanna's present that she had left behind. He sighed.

Robert and Joanna conversed minimally in the taxi. Andrea said nothing. They alighted the cab five minutes later, headed into the Savoy lobby and found a relatively quiet area to sit. Tea was organised for the Ferngroves, while Rossi had mineral water.

'Now, we can discuss our business,' said Rossi, sitting back comfortably in his seat. He lit a cigarette and offered the cigarette case towards Robert. Joanna beamed as if proud that Andrea was hers, while Robert, declining the offer, leaned forward eagerly.

'So, how is Guido?' He asked.

'Who?' said Rossi.

'Guido Zampelli, the bookseller in Venice.'

'How should I know this? I have met him only once, and that was sufficient.'

Robert was perplexed. 'I don't understand. You are here to discuss our arrangement for him to supply books to the shop, aren't you?'

'No! I am not a salesman,' said Rossi, displaying annoyance by exhaling loudly. 'I am here to retrieve something that he sold to you incorrectly.'

'But ...' It then became clear to Robert what Rossi was after. 'You mean the sketchbook?' Robert placed a quietly protective hand over his satchel. Joanna's expression became less carefree.

'That is correct. I am the rightful owner of that book. The Venetian bookseller had no right to sell it to you.' Rossi then went on to explain simply and assuredly how the book had passed through generations of his family and so was now his. His calm demeanour helped create an air of certainty about the matter, which Joanna thought plausible and Andrea's claim understandable. Robert, however, was having none of it.

'I'm sorry, Mr Rossi, but I bought the sketchbook in good faith from Zampelli. There was no suggestion of impropriety or illegality regarding the item. From what I understand, the then owner of the book gave it to him to sell.'

'That person was not the owner, only someone in possession of it.'

'I don't know how you can prove that. And, anyway, how do I know your supposed rights are legitimate?'

Rossi was beginning to feel angry, and he fought to contain his emotions. 'I do not lie,' he lied. 'That book was given to my ancient relative by the artist, and it has remained in our family as a treasured item ever since. All I wish to do is reinstate it into its proper place.' He stubbed out his cigarette with some force in the ashtray on the table.

'I don't wish to be rude, Mr Rossi, but if it was so treasured, how did it become lost and in the hands of a second-hand bookseller? No, I am satisfied that I am the book's rightful owner.'

An increasingly annoyed Rossi repeated it was improper for Ferngrove to hold this view, but Robert held firm in his position. Rossi tried a different approach.

'Then I will buy it from you. Mr Ferngrove. How much will you take for it?'

'It is not for sale.'

'But, Robbie,' chipped in Joanna, 'if the book belongs to Andrea, shouldn't he have it?'

'No.' The word was almost a snarl.

'Come, Mr Ferngrove, name your price. I am sure we can reach an agreement.'

'No.' The snarl came again. Robert grabbed his satchel and stood. 'I am leaving, Mr Rossi. There is nothing more to be said. Joanna?'

Joanna shook her head and stared down at her cold cup of tea. She felt she was betraying her brother but didn't think he was being particularly reasonable. Andrea had a point, didn't he?

To assuage his displeasure, Robert walked back to the shop at a good pace and reached it quickly. Jonathan showed surprise to see him back so soon and didn't like the stern expression he saw on Robert's reddened face.

'What's wrong? You look rather agitated.'

'Bloody cheek. That Rossi fellow wasn't here as Zampelli's representative at all. He was here to claim the sketchbook for himself.'

'What do you mean?' Jonathan heard the indignation in his partner's voice.

'You heard what I said. He says the sketchbook belongs to him.'

'Well, that's absurd. We bought it legitimately from that bookshop in Venice. He must be mistaken. What did he say?'

Robert recounted the discussion, calming slightly as he did so.

'Do you think he may have a claim on it?' asked Jonathan when Robert finished explaining events.

'Well, he may think so, but his story about it being a long-lost treasure is, frankly, ridiculous.'

'Is it, Robert? Are you sure? If I remember correctly, Zampelli didn't seem to know how the sketchbook came into his possession and didn't even appear to know what it was.'

'Don't you start! Joanna's already siding with Rossi, seemingly. Am I the only one that thinks he is making it all up?'

'Robert, just think about it for a moment. Why would he come here from Italy to claim the book if he were making up a story? He must believe that he has rights to it. How did he know the sketchbook even existed and know to look for it in Zampelli's shop? And do you think he knows anything about the special drawings?'

'I don't know, Jon, and frankly, I don't want to know. I bought the book. It is mine. I am keeping it. That's an end to it.'

'We bought the book, Robert. The two of us!' And, after a pause, 'let's go home. We'll close up early.'

'I feel I must apologise for Robert's behaviour, Andrea. He isn't normally like that. I don't know why he was so demonstrative. It is most unlike him.'

'Do not concern yourself, Joanna. I will talk to him again in the morning. He may be more reasonable, then. Now. You. Tomorrow, I will organise travel arrangements for Saturday and hotel accommodation in Milan. You will arrive in Milan on Sunday, and I will meet you at the railway station.'

'But, Andrea, I thought you were coming with me.' A rather alarmed Joanna said.

'No, I must return to Milan on Friday. You will be fine. The journey will be long, but you will be very comfortable. I shall see to that. You will be busy preparing for the journey tomorrow, as I, too, will be busy, so you will then come to the hotel for dinner in the evening. Yes?'

'Yes, Andrea.'

'My flight will leave the following morning, so we will say 'Arrivederci' that night. Now, you must go home, as I have things I must do this evening. Dinner will be here at seven-thirty. Okay?'

Compliantly, Joanna just said, 'Certainly, Andrea.'

The next morning, Andrea visited the Thomas Cook travel agency referred by the hotel concierge. Here, he booked his flight to Milan and arranged Joanna's trip for Saturday night. She would be travelling a long time, but at least she would be doing it in comfort and some style. She would leave from Victoria Station on the Night Ferry train, which would take her across the Channel and onto Paris, where the luxurious Trans Europe Express would complete her journey to Milan.

He also arranged with his friend, David, for Joanna to stay a few nights at his boutique hotel in the Corso

Monforte, a short distance from both his own apartment and the conservatorium. He would give the details to Joanna later that evening.

The only remaining thing for Andrea to do was to speak with Robert Ferngrove again about his property. He did not telephone the shop, deciding instead to simply appear there, creating an element of surprise that he believed would work to his advantage.

So, at two o'clock, Andrea Rossi again entered the Cecil Court shop.

'Good afternoon, gentlemen.' Andrea Rossi announced as he moved past the displays toward Robert and Jonathan at the rear. Robert particularly didn't seem pleased to see him. Jonathan stood close to his partner in greeting the Italian. Both were a little apprehensive.

'Good afternoon, Mr Rossi,' said Robert. 'Is there anything more I can help you with other than what we discussed yesterday?'

'Yes, Mr Ferngrove. I wish to give you one thousand of your British pounds for the sketchbook. I can arrange for a banker's draft to be with you within the hour. What do you say?'

Jonathan's face displayed a mix of delight and shock. That is an awful lot of money. He thought. Surely, Robert would take it? Rossi moved to light a cigarette.

'Please. No smoking in here, and I'm sorry, Mr Rossi. As I keep telling you, it is not for sale.'

'But Robert!' Jonathan whispered. Robert shook his head.

Rossi placed the cigarette case and lighter back into his jacket pocket. 'One thousand, two hundred. That is my last offer.'

Before Robert could say anything further, Jonathan interjected, 'That is a generous offer, Mr Rossi. Please allow my partner and me a moment to consider it.' Robert shot Jonathan an unpleasant look.

'I shall take a walk in this court and return in just ten minutes. I must have time to get to my bank.' With that, Andrea Rossi left the shop.

'Robert! One thousand, two hundred pounds. That is a huge amount of money. It would take us months to earn that. We could really develop the business with it, and …'

'Just stop, Jon. I understand what you are saying, but I won't do it. I simply can't. I have come to realise that this is not something I have a choice about. From the first day we discovered it in the Venice bookshop, it has somehow cast a spell on me.'

Robert had begun to believe that it was, at first, Turner's exquisite craftsmanship that captivated him. The simple pencil sketches of Venice, its history, its canals, its people, but day by day the lure of the sketches of Byron in captivating sexual detail drew him in deeper, tracing the lines and curves of his subjects with his eyes and his fingers. They were hypnotic.

At every possible moment he found himself bringing the battered old book to the dining table and devouring those two special sketches. He had begun to believe the sketchbook held something essential; some message perhaps that was just out of his grasp but would become clear to him the more he delved into those salon scenes.

Jonathan found it hard to comprehend what Robert was feeling and had just said. He had always been the sensible and logical one. This was so alien. He knew, however, that Robert meant just what he said. He wouldn't sell it, and he, Jonathan, would have to accept that situation, as he would the fact that the sketchbook was, in Robert's mind, not a joint ownership but his solely, and that saddened Jonathan.

'But Robert, the money!'

'Yes, I know, Jon. I'm sorry, but I can't sell it.'

Jonathan knew there was no point in continuing to argue his point. Robert's mind was set, and there was no shifting it when that happened. He would simply have to be resigned to the fact. They waited in silence for Rossi's return.

'Well?' Rossi's impatience was beginning to simmer. 'What is your answer?'

'The answer is as it was before. It is not for sale.'

'You will regret this,' Rossi snarled at Robert, then glowered at Jonathan. 'You both will regret the decision. I have ways of making you want to change your minds. You will not find those ways pleasant. Be warned. Be afraid.' With great deliberation, he turned from the two men and moved toward the door. 'I mean what I say.' And then he was gone.

'Be afraid.' Jonathan almost choked on the threat. 'There's not much chance that I won't. God, Robert, what have you done? He was furious. What do you think he meant? What shall we do? What will he do? Is it safe here? Should we move?'

'Jonathan. Stop it. You're getting hysterical. He's going back to Italy soon, so it's all bluster. He can't do anything to us. He's just angry that he couldn't get the sketchbook. He'll get over it.'

'I hope you're right, Robert. I really do.'

Andrea Rossi wasn't angry. He was livid.

Chapter Seven

Andrea sat at the crisply dressed table, the soft glow of the chandelier above reflecting the polished silverware, crystal glass and white linen tablecloth, as befitting a hotel of this stature. The restaurant ambience – voices low, laughter restrained – wrapped round him, heightening the sense of anticipation that had settled in his chest. He checked his watch, then looked up just as the maître d' appeared at the entrance, holding the door with a practiced flourish. Joanna was on time. He was pleased.

She stepped inside, her presence immediately drawing the eye. The black dress she wore was the very definition of understated elegance: its lines perfectly tailored, emphasizing her delicate frame and the effortless grace with which she moved. She paused for a moment, scanning the room, before the maître d' inclined his head and gestured toward Andrea's table, following discreetly behind her.

Andrea watched her approach, every detail amplified in his awareness—the snug fit of her dress caressing her body with each step, the subtle, confident smile that played at her lips, the way the seductive light stroked the curve of her neck and shoulders. There was a quiet sensuality in the way she moved, an assurance that seemed to set her apart from everyone else in the room. She did not hurry, nor did she falter; her footsteps, muffled by thick carpeting, suggested she was entirely at home in this world of understated luxury.

As she drew closer, Andrea felt time slow down. The clinking of glasses, the low murmur of conversation faded into a distant hum. He realized he was holding his breath, captivated by her poise, her beauty, and the magnetic pull she exerted without effort. When at last she reached his table and their eyes met, a spark passed between them – he had never experienced anything like this. And he hadn't seen this Joanna now standing before him either. He wasn't sure how he felt about this. Was he captivated by her or was he angry at himself over how she was making him feel? He stood.

'Joanna, you look beautiful. Please be seated.'

The maître d' drew a chair from the table awaiting her move towards it. 'Thank you, Andrea. This is all rather lovely.'

They sat and the sommelier poured two flutes of champagne. 'To success!' Andrea toasted.

She declined Rossi's offer of a cigarette and, no, she didn't mind if he smoked. 'I think there is something very manly about a man who smokes,' she told him.

After leaving Robert Ferngrove yesterday afternoon in his incensed state, Andrea Rossi had contacted his associate, Sarah Mulholland, and met with her at her home and business premises in Belgravia. Miss Mulholland had helped him through some deals in England previously and, provided there was a sizeable commission for her, she hadn't asked questions about any of them. Rossi's latest proposal was to be no different.

He required her to have one or two of her employees visit the Cecil Court shop to let Ferngrove and Spencer know the seriousness of their predicament. Rossi learned from her several days later, while he was back in Milan, that the body of a woman had been discovered in the antique shop doorway adjacent to Ferngrove and Spencer's shop. Bow Street police detectives found it was the body of the shop owner's assistant. The shock among all the retailers in the Court had been palpable. A 'calling' card had been attached to Ferngrove and Spencer's front door. It read, BE AFRAID. Mrs Mulholland had taken a 'subtle' approach to creating fear in the two men.

Joanna's shoulder-length auburn hair framed a face that Rossi noticed wore minimal make-up. The effect was startling on him. He knew she was a good-looking woman, but he wasn't prepared for her sensuality. Her grey-green eyes were bright and lively.

'Everything is booked for you, Joanna, but I'm afraid it will be a strenuous twenty-four hours. At least you will do it in style and comfort.' He went on to explain that the train would leave Victoria Station at 10 pm on Saturday, and she would be able to take her cello and luggage on board with her and into her private sleeper cabin. She would, he continued, arrive at Gare du Nord, Paris, a little before 9 am, leaving her an hour – plenty of time – to get to Gare de Lyon, from where the Trans Europe Express would take her to Milan.

'I shall meet your train at the station, Joanna, when the train arrives at seven p.m. You will enjoy the trip. It is all first class. I have also organised your hotel for the five nights you will be in the city. It is a pleasant hotel near to where you will practise and have your audition. We will collect the itinerary I wrote for you from my hotel room, after our dinner.'

Not for the first time, Joanna was dumbfounded. 'Andrea, I really don't know what to say. What you are doing for me is incredible.'

'As I have said before, Joanna, it is my pleasure to do this for you.'

After a wonderful meal, they went to Andrea's room, where more champagne waited on ice. In the lift, he had felt Joanna leaning into him and gazing at his face, her eyes wide and pupils dilated. She had bitten and licked her lips while listening intently to what he was saying, or so he thought.

Seated opposite Andrea in the room, champagne in hand, she again showed signs of listening to him, leaning forward, her legs slightly apart. It was then that Andrea realised what was different about her that evening.

'I want to show you my gratitude,' Joanna said in a quiet and sultry voice. She put down her glass and moved beside Andrea.

'You don't need to do that, Joanna.'

'But that's where you're wrong, Andrea. I do, and I am going to.' She slipped the dress from her shoulders. 'Right now.'

After they had dressed a while later, Andrea handed Joanna the documents, the itinerary he had written, and a generous amount of cash for her journey. He didn't even consider the possibility that she may have considered the cash humiliating following her lovemaking with him.

'Well, Joanna, you are all set for Saturday, and I must be up early tomorrow for my flight home, so we will say 'arrivederci' until I see you on Sunday evening.'

He let her kiss his lips gently before she smiled and headed for the door.

'Ciao, Andrea.'

'Ciao, Joanna.'

With Rossi on his way back to Italy, Joanna visited the shop to let Robert know what was happening. Entering the Court, she literally bumped into Elsie, the assistant at the antique shop next door to their shop.

'Gosh, sorry, Elsie. I didn't see you. My mind's elsewhere today.' It would be the last time she spoke to her.

The shop, like the Court, was rather crowded, she thought, mainly with tourists. She went to the back and saw her musical score lying there. She put her bag down and went to help Robert and Jonathan with the customers.

When there were only two browsers left, she retired to the back of the shop and waited for Robert to join her.

'Well, Robbie, everything's set. I head off tomorrow. I'm so excited.' She gave him details of her itinerary, and Robert wrote it down.

'Where's Rossi?'

'Andrea left for Milan this morning.'

'So, he's gone, then?'

'Yes, Robbie, I said so. Why are you so tense?'

'I'm fine, Jo. Sorry. We've just been so busy this morning. I must say, your travel arrangements look fabulous. Will you have any trouble getting the cello on board?'

'Not at all, and I have rehearsals, and the audition all lined up. I'm very excited.'

He laughed. 'Yes. So you said. I do hope it goes well for you, sis.'

Joanna picked up her score, kissed Robert and, waving at Jonathan, left the shop. She wondered how on earth she would pass the time until tomorrow evening. All her packing was done. She had written to her parents in some detail about her wonderful opportunity. Perhaps she could help Lucy clear the flat up in readiness for Susie's arrival. The girls all had dinner at the flat that night, and the next day, Joanna mooched around, the time absolutely refusing to move any faster. She repacked her suitcase, tried to read, ensured the cello was safe and happy, played a record, ate lunch – not much – checked her documentation again, and wandered around fidgeting and feeling restless. Eventually, the time came when she could stand the wait no longer, and while there were still over three hours to go before her train left, she decided it would be better to actually be on her way rather than sit around here.

Lucy helped her and her belongings into the taxi, and she headed off to Victoria Station. When she arrived, she was pleasantly surprised to find the train waiting at platform 2. She underwent the Customs checks before being shown to her single compartment. It was extremely comfortable, with plenty of safe room for her cello. Joanna knew this was going to be a glorious trip!

She was not mistaken. The train departed precisely at ten o'clock, and by eleven-thirty, after the steward had collected her breakfast order card, the metronomic clickety-clack had lulled Joanna into a calm and restful sleep. She didn't hear the train being loaded onto the ferry at Dover at 12.35 am, nor it being off-loaded at Dunkerque at 4.30 am. It was only the gentle tapping at the door at 6 am that woke her.

The steward wheeled in her breakfast trolley, the aroma of freshly brewed coffee preceding the sight of her ordered meal. She ate at the cabin's foldable table. *I could get used to this;* she smiled to herself.

After breakfast, Joanna washed and changed into the day's travelling clothes. She felt a special need to dress well, given she would be on the even more opulent Trans Europe Express in just a few hours.

Feeling just a little sad at leaving the train in Paris, she looked forward, however, to reaching the Gare du Lyon for her next stage of the journey.

If she thought the first train journey was good, she was going to be shocked at how splendid the Paris-to-Milan leg was. It was first class only, with a limited number of seats providing spacious legroom. The dining car was immaculate, with just 54 places. Impressive! She loved it and was desperately sorry to reach her destination, Milan Porta Garibaldi Station, some seven hours later, although this was tempered considerably by the thought of seeing Andrea again.

Joanna alighted the train, which was ten minutes later than scheduled, and a porter helped her with her luggage while she looked after her cello. Tipping the porter at the end of the platform, she looked eagerly around the newly built station for Andrea, but she couldn't see him. She wasn't unduly worried but had concerns about the possibility of pickpockets coming her way. She had been forewarned about them. A further ten minutes passed. Her eagerness and excitement waned slightly. When yet another ten minutes went by, Joanna began to feel anxious.

She felt herself extremely conspicuous, standing alone near the station concourse. There weren't many people about at this time on a Sunday evening, and she was wary of those who, like her, stood around, waiting for what? She didn't know.

What if he doesn't show up? she asked herself, hoped it was rhetorical. But then, *what could have happened to him? 'Where is he?*

A gust of wind snatched at her skirt, and she began to notice things hitherto unseen: the dark shadows in the corners of the station and the lack of station officials or police. Her eyes scanned for anything that would ease her mounting anxiety.

A small, unkempt-looking man headed towards her. His walk was slow and deliberate. Joanna clutched her handbag and brought the cello closer to her side, her knuckles whitening. He stopped a few feet away and looked at her, then slowly put his hand inside his jacket. She held her breath. The man pulled out what looked to her like a pale envelope. The man moved close. He held the object out towards her and, in poor English, said, 'Mees Fengro?'

'Yes,' she hesitatingly replied.

'Meesta Rossi say come.'

She took the still proffered envelope from the man and opened it.

'Joanna, I am so sorry I am held up. Trust this man, he will take you to the hotel. I will be there soon. Andrea.'

Relief flooded Joanna, and for a moment, her knees felt too weak to hold her up. She nodded mutely and let him pick up her bag, but not the cello. They set off for the exit, she struggling to keep pace with the little Italian.

Out through the station doors, they headed towards a car. The man placed her luggage in the boot and gestured toward the cello. Joanna shook her head, pointing to the passenger door, which he opened, and through which she struggled to put her instrument on the back seat of the Fiat. She sat in the front passenger seat. As he pulled away from the kerb, the nervous tension drained from her, replaced by a wave of relief and fatigue.

They reached the hotel in just a few minutes. The driver helped Joanna out of the car and indicated the entrance to the foyer. He reached into the rear seat for the cello and passed it to her. He then collected her suitcase and followed her inside.

The manager, David Sala, was waiting in the lobby to greet Joanna. Andrea Rossi's friend was warm and welcoming, and she was soon in her room unpacking, still wondering what had happened to Andrea.

It was still early in the evening. She had eaten well on the train – very well, in fact – and wasn't tired. There was nothing to do, and while it was still light outside, the weather didn't entice her. Anyway, she told herself, she should wait here for Andrea, or, rather, she would wait in the hotel bar near the lobby, which is where she was when he came through the hotel entrance.

She again saw the undeniable presence he exuded. He moved with a deliberate grace, each step measured and purposeful. He never seemed flustered and had an air of authority about him. Joanna waved to him from the bar, and he met her gaze with a calmness that seemed to project a quiet power, reliable but simultaneously daunting.

He kissed her cheek formally. 'I am sorry that I could not meet you as I had said I would, but I had some business to attend to.'

This greeting confused Joanna. She believed they were on more intimate terms than a mere peck on the cheek deserved, but she said nothing to Andrea about her feelings.

'That is fine, Andrea. You are here now, and that is what matters.'

He didn't offer an explanation, and she didn't ask.

'I cannot stay very long, I regret, but we will have a lot of time over the coming days. Tomorrow, I will show you the conservatoire and where you can rehearse. I will introduce you to the director of the orchestra, and then we will see a little of my city. Is that all right with you?'

'But, yes, of course, Andrea.'

'Good, then I shall collect you at nine o'clock tomorrow morning. Do you have everything you want? If there is anything, just ask David, the manager, and he will take care of it for you. Until tomorrow then, good night, Joanna.'

And he was gone.

She felt dazed and let down. She had been so looking forward to seeing Andrea again, but this sudden stiffness was not what she expected at all.

Don't be so ridiculous, she told herself. *If he was abrupt, he obviously had his reasons. Just remember where you are and what you're doing.* She ordered another drink and felt much better about herself.

The next morning, he was true to his word, waiting for Joanna in the hotel lobby.

'Good morning, Joanna. We have a busy day today. I hope you slept well last evening.' He made no move to kiss her.

'Good morning to you too, Andrea. I did, thank you, and I'm looking forward to whatever today brings, especially seeing the conservatoire.'

That is what they did that day. Andrea and the director showed Joanna around the complex and reserved a rehearsal room for her for the next two mornings. They explained access to her, and they visited the auditorium. Little did she realise that all the while, she was being assessed for her character suitability. The audition time was determined for 11 a.m. on Thursday in the auditorium, and then it was over. She left with Andrea for a little sightseeing and relaxation.

Joanna was satisfied with her preparations and felt confident about the audition. She knew Andrea said she would get a place in the orchestra, but she wanted to prove she was worthy; to get the post on merit. And so it proved.

'You are good enough to be principal cello, Joanna, but for political reasons, I must start you in the ranks, but in the front desks. I cannot create difficulties in the section by placing you ahead of the others, but once they see and hear you play, you will soon be principal.'

The director's comments had delighted Joanna after the audition was over. The pay and conditions, the scheduled programme of events for the coming season, and all other 'housekeeping' matters were equally satisfactory and would be incorporated into the contract that Andrea would bring to her later that afternoon.

'Welcome to the Angelicum Orchestra of Milan.'

Back in her hotel room, she telephoned Andrea's office to tell him the news.

'Of course, Joanna,' he gloated. 'I told you that you would get the post.'

'Yes, you did, you lovely man, but the director told me I got it because of my skill, which is wonderful.'

'Roberto is a very astute director. He knows the correct things to say.'

'He said you would have my contract later today.'

'Yes, it will be delivered to me, and then I will bring it with me when we go out to dinner to celebrate this evening.'

'How wonderful! Thank you, Andrea. Are we going somewhere nice?'

'A restaurant close to the Duomo, and we shall go past La Scala. So, a special place for a special occasion. I will collect you from your hotel at seven-thirty. Ciao.'

Again, she felt there was this abruptness. It was somewhat disarming for her. It seemed to Joanna as if she were being enticed into a beautiful world where all things were gorgeous, and she was immersed in its splendour. Then to find the world became distorted, misshapen, diaphanous and she couldn't escape. Trapped. But, once more, she told herself not to be so foolish and unappreciative of what Andrea had done for her and what, seemingly, he was to continue to do. *For me*, she told herself. *For me!* And shrugged off these ungrateful feelings of doubt.

The restaurant was perfect. Its surroundings, the ambience, service, food, wine were all of exceptional quality and she, Joanna, was very much a part of it. The contract had been signed, so she was joyously committed now.

'This is sublime, Andrea. Do you eat here often?'

'Occasionally, but only with a beautiful woman. You know, Joanna, you look very much like your brother. I have just now seen how similar you are.'

'Oh, heavens, not too much, I hope,' she giggled, realising how tipsy she was feeling: adrenaline, excitement, wine. 'We have shared interests, that's for sure. Art, mushic. Oops, sorry, music.' She giggled again. 'He'sh a lovely man, has always looked out for me, and, of courshe, I've been supportive of Robert in all he's done, even when our parents dishapproved.'

'Disapproved? When was that?'

'When he and Jona…, Jonathan became partners. Oh gosh, Andrea, I'm feeling a bit sloshed.'

'I'm not surprised, Joanna. Everything is catching up with you.' Andrea smiled. 'But tell me, why would your parents disapprove of them opening the bookshop?'

'Not that, silly. Living together. Sharing the flat. Being in love.'

Andrea was astounded at what she had just said. He couldn't believe it. 'You mean … they are … homosexual?' he whispered.

'Yes, of course. That's all right, isn't it? They're very discreet,' she slurred.

'In this country, Joanna, such activity is considered to be against the teaching of our Catholic faith. It is thought to be disgusting, perverted …'

'But you don't think that do you, Andrea? Do you?'

'I think we should not talk more about this. I will get you to your hotel.'

'Oh, Andrea. I haven't angered you, have I? You're not angry? Say you're not. Hmm?'

'You do not anger me, Joanna. I am pleased you have been so honest with me.'

'Well, that's all right, then. I need the restroom. Excushe me.'

Joanna didn't remember getting back to her hotel room, nor when or where Andrea had left. She knew she was extremely tired. She somehow managed to get out of her clothes and fell, giggling, into her bed.

The next morning, she felt surprisingly alert and, after showering and a number of cups of coffee, ready to face the day. It had been a fabulous night, a fabulous end to a fabulous week. She did recall that Andrea was picking her up at eleven to take her cello to his flat before showing her the apartment he had picked out for her while she was in Milan. After that, she would be heading home on Saturday to collect the rest of her belongings and then returning for the orchestra engagements in just under a week's time. She was hesitant about leaving her cello, but it was preferable to trying to get it safely onto an aeroplane, and after all, she was coming straight back to Milan. And it would give her a chance to see where Andrea lived and see where her new home was, and that prospect she found exciting.

She was ready when he called her from the lobby.

Chapter Eight

A damp chill hung in the air as Robert moved to unlock the shop door. The Monday morning mist clung to the Court's cobblestones like a shroud. There was every likelihood that by the afternoon, the mist would have grown into, at best, a fog or, more probably, that awful smog. The shadow of last Thursday's encounter with Rossi remained burdensome to Robert Ferngrove.

A police officer stopped Robert and Jonathan as they entered the Court, questioning them as to why they were there and who they were. Having satisfied the officer of their credentials, they learned that Mrs Hatton, the antique dealer's assistant, had that morning been found dead in the adjacent shop's doorway. The news was like a punch to the gut. Robert thought of her jovial laughter as she'd bartered over antique teacups, now a horrifying memory.

Shocked, they were allowed to enter their premises but told to wait inside, as it was probable that a senior police officer would wish to interview them. Purely routine, of course.

'When had it happened, officer?'

The reply was what was normal in circumstances such as these: non-informational and non-committal.

As Robert moved to unlock the shop's door, he noticed a small card wedged into the shop doorframe. It read, BE AFRAID. Just two words, but their stark simplicity sent shivers down his spine. It didn't occur to either of them that the card could have had any link to the incident next door. Rossi couldn't be blamed for Mrs Hatton's sudden demise. He was in Italy.

Robert removed the card, opened the door, and entered the shop. He laid the card on the bench at the back of the shop. Jonathan's normally cheerful face was etched with worry, paced the narrow space behind the counter. He stopped, his eyes again landing on the small card that now lay prostrate and menacing on the bench.

He picked it up with trembling fingers, his brow furrowed. 'This is serious, Robert,' he said, his voice marginally above a whisper. 'What if he's behind all this?'

'But Rossi has left England, hasn't he?' Robert said. 'This threat from him was just that – a warning to us about his demands for the sketchbook – nothing more sinister.'

'Should we show the card to the police?' a panicked Jonathan asked.

'You know we can't do that,' Robert whispered, as if walls had ears. 'They wouldn't take us seriously. Threats to a disgruntled bookseller? And, more importantly, they may look into who we are.'

Robert recognised in Jonathan's demeanour that, though scared, he knew Robert was right. Even mentioning Rossi's veiled threats would sound like the ramblings of two overworked bookworms. Yet, silence felt like complicity. And the thought of them being investigated was even worse. Jonathan rubbed his temples, the weight of the situation pressing down on him. 'Then what do we do?' he asked, his voice hoarse. 'Live in fear every day?'

'No, I will not live like that, Jonathan. We have enough to be wary of in our lives as it is. I think we should just see how things go. Keep as quiet as we can and hope it is just Rossi's frustrated belligerence. And, with the police in the Court for a while, there won't be any customers about, so any further visit from whoever is responsible is unlikely. What do you think?'

Jonathan looked up, and Robert saw the concern flickering in his eyes. 'It's dangerous, Robert,' he said, his voice hesitant.

'I know,' Robert sighs, the weight of the decision settling on him. 'But what other choice do we have?'

A flicker of resolve replaced the fear in Robert's eyes. 'We'll be strong for each other,' he said. 'We will answer any questions that the police ask in relation to the incident next door, but our issue with Rossi should remain our secret.'

Neither of them knew if this was foolhardy or offered a glimmer of hope. But in the face of fear, they had only each other and the desperate need to protect the life they knew, the real life nestled amongst the fiction lining their shelves.

Time dragged on as they waited to be spoken to by the police. They watched what little activity there was out in the Court and heard muffled voices, banging and movement from next door but nothing more.

After what seemed an eternity, a man in a raincoat, its collar turned up against the worsening fog and a trilby hat, entered the shop together with another similarly dressed younger, hatless man. The older of the two men brandished a police warrant card at Robert and Jonathan and introduced himself as Detective Sergeant Dagg and his associate as Detective Constable Cole. He proceeded to ask them a series of what he described as routine questions, the answers to which DC Cole wrote in his notebook: their names, addresses, whereabouts earlier that morning, and what they knew of the deceased.

Robert was rather worried when they both gave the same address, but neither of the police officers commented or questioned the information. 'Had they noticed anyone acting oddly in the Court over the last few days?' To which they replied in the negative. And that was it, other than an 'if you think of anything that might assist us in our enquiries ...'

Jonathan had been a bundle of nerves during this questioning and was now shaking with relief. Robert put a comforting hand on his, smiling as he looked into Jonathan's eyes. It seemed to help.

With the Court now out of bounds to general traffic, they decided it wasn't worth staying open, so they closed the shop and, after advising the bobby on duty at the entrance to the thoroughfare of their actions, left for home.

They returned to the Court the next day only to be stopped once more by the same police officer at the entrance to the thoroughfare. 'I'm sorry, gentlemen, but the whole court is closed today.'

'How long will it be before we can come back in?'

'Impossible to say, sir. Do we have your contact details? If so, we will contact you when you may enter your premises. Do either of you have a telephone connected in your homes?'

'No, officer. But if someone would get a message to me in flat 5, that would be very kind,' a quick-minded Robert said. 'Jonathan and I live in the same block of flats, so I can let him know. Is that all right with you, Jonathan?'

'Er, yes, yes, that's fine, Robert. Thanks.'

'Right you are, sir. I'll let the appropriate officer know that.'

The two men then left for home. 'That was clever of you, Robert.'

It was Thursday morning when the knock came at flat 5, 33 Ufford Street. A young, helmeted policeman saluted Robert as he opened the door and told him it was now permissible to return to Cecil Court whenever convenient. Robert thanked him and closed the door.

Robert, watching from the shop, was awestruck by the sheer number of people swarming the Court that day. They did very little business, however, and it was clear the visitors were interested only in the ghoulish act of seeing where the now-publicised incident had taken place. The next day, the Court was back to its normal level of activity, the sightseers having, in the main, satisfied their vulturous appetites.

That afternoon, the editors at the Evening Standard had obviously felt that with no arrest or exciting development, the Cecil Court story was no longer front-page news. A brief reference to the matter appeared now only on the third page, low down. In its place, readers learned more about the activities of two violent east-end London gangsters: Reginald and Ronald Kray.

When a beaming Joanna Ferngrove walked into the shop the following Monday morning, Robert was both delighted and relieved.

'Jo! I didn't know you were back.'

'I'm not. Well, obviously, I am, but, hopefully, I'm flying back to Milan this afternoon, as long as this weather doesn't stop me. I only came back to collect the last of my belongings from the flat.'

'Is he with you?'

'If by 'he' you mean Andrea, then, no, he isn't. I do wish you'd be kinder about him. He's looking after me so well. He's even found me a place to live.'

'I take it, then, the audition was a success?'

'Yes, it was, Robbie, amazingly so, and that's why I need to get back. The orchestra has publicity engagements coming up that I have to be part of, plus I've got to get settled into my new home. Oh, here's the address, and it has a phone. Here's the number too.' Joanna fished out a sheet of paper with the details on it from her handbag and passed it over to her brother. 'Gosh, Robbie, it's all happening so wonderfully quickly. It's a whirlwind.'

'This has all happened so quickly for you. Are you absolutely sure it's what you want? No doubts?'

I've thought it over carefully on the trip over there and I admit I have asked myself that again and again, but I've got a place in an orchestra – a first-rate orchestra at that – and that overrides any doubts. You know how hard it's been for me to get a posting at all, so this dispel any concerns I may have had. It's an opportunity I just can't pass up.'

Robert nodded his understanding of how important the posting was to his sister.

'Are you okay?' She continued.

'Yes, we're okay.' And after a brief pause: 'Did you hear about what happened to poor Mrs Hatton? Found dead in the antique shop doorway.'

'Oh God, Robbie. When? How?'

'Last Monday. The police cordoned off the Court, but we haven't heard anything more. We don't know if she had a heart attack or whether she suffered some sort of assault, and there's nothing recent in the paper. But. When we came to the shop that morning, this card was stuck in our door jamb.' He showed Joanna the BE AFRAID card.

'What does it mean? Is it to do with Mrs Hatton?'

'We don't know, but I think it was from Rossi.'

'What!' Joanna exclaimed. 'For God's sake, Robbie, how can that possibly be? Andrea was with me in Milan on Monday. He met me there.'

'I don't know, Jo, but it was the same threat that he made about the sketchbook before he left.'

'Oh, come on, Robbie. You have got to stop this bad-mouthing of Andrea. He is not the ogre you are making him out to be.'

'Perhaps. For your sake, I'll try to be more considerate.' He said without feeling convinced.

'Thank you, darling. Well, I must be off. So much still to do. I don't know when I'll be back next. I'll send word when I know.' And after a quick peck on Robert's cheek and a wave to Jonathan, she was gone.

For the next two weeks, Robert and Jonathan kept a lower-than-normal profile, both at home and in the shop. The police did not disturb them any further, and nor did they hear anything more about the death.

They spent their evenings happily at home, although Jonathan expressed serious concerns about Robert's seeming obsession with the Turner sketches. Not all the magnificent Venice sketches, however, but the two sexually explicit ones of Byron. He pored over them, his eyes devouring the eroticism and languishing in the lure of the scenes. Jonathan was excluded from enjoying the sketchbook by his partner. Whenever he made a move to sit beside Robert and admire the sketches, Robert would not permit him to see the Byron sketches at all, closing the book with care each time saying nothing to his partner.

There were previous times when Jonathan had raised the matter of them sharing and enjoying the book only to receive Robert's gentle but firm rebuke and a reminder that the sketchbook was his, not theirs, something, Robert realised, that Jonathan found hard to accept, but would have to come to terms with. He seemed oblivious to the possibility that his possessiveness about the book might be creating a wedge between them. He should have been more attuned to Jonathan's worries that it could be.

When the invitation came in the mail from Lord Peter Henderson, a friend from their early times in London, to attend the salubrious Rockingham Club in Archer Street to celebrate his fiftieth birthday, it was almost a relief to be taken out of their solicitude to rejoin life once again, and an even greater pleasure to be going to a club considered to be one of London's most exclusive queer societies, attracting persons of great standing and education. The date of the function was soon – Friday, 20 October – and they both knew that the party would be quite riotous and not a little bawdy. Letting their hair down was just what they needed after the last couple of weeks. The RSVP was answered immediately.

Chapter Nine

'I think it's time I visited Mother again,' announced Jonathan. 'Things have quietened down on the Rossi front as well as customers as usual at this time of year, so I thought I'd take the opportunity to see her. It's been a few days since I visited, and I'm feeling a bit guilty.'

'Fair enough, Jon. We do have a bit to do on the mail orders, but nothing that can't be managed. How long will you be there? Don't forget Peter's birthday party on Friday.'

'Oh heavens, only for the day, Robert. I thought perhaps tomorrow. What do you think?'

'That's fine. She'll be delighted to see you again. You make me feel bad about not visiting my parents. I'll organise something on that front in the new year. We can go for a holiday, though Father won't allow us both in the house, and that is why I find it hard to see them. I feel sorry for Mother. Perhaps I'll invite her up to town for a few days.'

'Good idea. I like your mum.'

'You like everyone, Jon.' Robert teases.

'Ooh, I don't know about that.'

The next day, they set off as usual from their Southwark flat, walking the half mile to Waterloo Station. When the weather was fine, they could make the journey in eleven minutes. This day was grey and slightly chilly. They reached the station in fourteen minutes and went their different ways.

Robert made for the Northern Line tube while Jonathan followed his regular route to the mainline platforms for the train to Earlsfield Station. Neither of them had noticed the young man in the donkey jacket. If they had, they might have recognised him as the person who had followed them from Cecil Court to their home the day before and who was maintaining a discreet distance behind them this morning.

He hadn't spent all night outside the block of flats but had found out which flat Robert Ferngrove lived in from the list of names displayed on the intercom buzzer before another man had undertaken the 'night shift' observation. As ordered, he was back on the scene early that day, grateful for the café across the road where he could keep warm and keep watch through the steamed-up window.

It was Jonathan that he decided to tag at Waterloo. Standing right behind him at the ticket office, he heard Jonathan ask for a single to Earlsfield, and he did likewise.

Jonathan was unaware of this man. He didn't know they shared the same carriage on the multi-unit train. Nor did he see him get off it at the same time he did. He was unaware of being followed along Penwith Road and was oblivious to the man watching him go through the gate at number thirteen Whatmore Street and be greeted and welcomed in by his mother.

The man added this address to his notebook. Now he had three addresses for the booksellers. The man left this suburban street to report his findings to his employer in Belgravia.

The Rockingham Club in Archer Street was a gentleman's club. It had Regency-style striped wallpaper, wood-panelled walls, leather sofas and chairs, and a white grand piano. It exuded respectability and wealth. The dress code was strict and formal. The club's clientele paid hefty subscriptions, and as a result, its membership comprised the well-to-do, including aristocracy, politicians, and professional men.

Conforming to expectations of social propriety and restraint, middle-class affluent men leveraged their societal advantages to build discreet yet far-reaching social networks within private clubs such as the Rockingham. There was, however, more to the club than first met the eye, for its pomp and glamour were covers for the fact that this was a queer gentleman's club where homosexual men could get together to dine, drink and dance without fear of reprisals. The club did have its ladies' night on Sundays, but the rest of the week was devoted solely to the discerning male.

It was known, of course, to the police, but wealth, privilege and influence were major factors in their 'blind-eyes' to the goings on there, provided it was kept inside the club and not spill out from its oaken doors.

Robert and Jonathan arrived at the designated time on Friday evening, dressed splendidly yet understated in their black, single-breasted evening jackets and black ties. It had been a while since they had dressed up for an occasion, and they felt especially glamorous. They loved the ambience of the Club, presenting their invitation to the doorman upon entering. Peter Henderson saw them enter and sauntered over to greet them.

'So nice to see you both again,' he said as he kissed the cheeks of both men. 'Thank you very much for coming. How are you both? Robert?'

'I'm well, my Lord. We're well.' Robert answered, correcting himself.

'None of this milord stuff. It's Peter, as you ruddy well know.'

'Yes, of course, Peter.'

'Happy birthday,' announced Jonathan, 'we have a little something for you,' handing over an exquisitely wrapped package.

'How lovely. Thank you. Thank you both. May I open it now?' Taking it from Jonathan.

'Yes, please do.'

Carefully untying the pink ribbon of the package and unfolding the charming green paper, Lord Henderson gave a slight gasp of pleasure to see a volume of Rupert Brooke poems.

'How wonderful! I know his family, you know. This is lovely. How kind. Come on through and meet the rest of the boys,' he cooed, handing the present on to one of the club's service staff. 'Look after this for me, Tommy, please.'

The clubrooms were already busy with activity. 'Here, everyone, say hello to two of my delightful friends, Robert and Jonathan.' Both men were handed a glass of champagne, and the pleasantries of introductions began.

The two men met two young aristocrats – neighbours of Peter's in Oxfordshire in town for the occasion – a barrister; a member of parliament and a government official. None of the new acquaintances were aware of the Cecil Court bookshop and were keen to learn more about it, promising to visit as soon as possible.

Peter floated between all of his guests, being the perfect bon vivant and host, ensuring everyone had everything they wanted, and reminding those who were interested about the private rooms along the corridor past the toilets, to which much tittering occurred. And so it went on throughout the evening, which, to Robert and Jonathan, seemed to end all too soon, having made some wonderful friends with whom they promised to stay in touch.

On the return home in the taxi at around 1 a.m., they felt relaxed and happy and perhaps just a little tipsy. It was quite warm inside the cab, and the rain that had begun to fall made their cocoon rather cosy. They cuddled up in silent accompaniment.

They alighted the taxi outside their block of flats and bade the driver a very good night before hurrying over to and unlocking the entrance door to the building's flats. As they ascended the stairs towards their front door, Jonathan said nervously, 'Something doesn't feel right, Rob.'

The door was locked as it should be, and there didn't appear to be anything out of the ordinary as Robert turned the key. Jonathan was clinging to Robert's left arm as they entered the room, and the overhead light switched on.

And there it was, the cause of Jonathan's unease, laying atop the elegant Edwardian chestnut hall table with its hand-carved turned legs – a peacock feather.

They both stood motionless, staring down at it.

'Did you put that there?' An incredulous Jonathan asked his partner with some concern. 'I didn't see you do it.'

'I was going to ask you the same question, Jon.'

'But ... I don't understand, Rob. How did it get here?' Robert sensed that Jonathan was becoming overanxious.

'I don't know.' Then, slowly, the thought came to Robert, although he was reluctant to voice it, that someone had entered their home and placed it there. 'Have a look around, Jon. Do you see anything else odd?'

They both gazed about the room. Nothing appeared out of the ordinary.

'No, nothing that I can see.'

'Don't be alarmed, Jon, but I think someone has been here.'

'What? Who? How? Why?'

Robert moved about the room, not wanting to trust his eyes, checking on everything of value and the windows. All seemed in order. He hurried to the main bedroom. Again, everything appeared normal. He opened the wardrobe door where the small safe was and checked inside. The sketchbook lay there as he had left it earlier.

Jonathan, meanwhile, nervously checked the other rooms – kitchen, second bedroom – nothing seemed amiss there either.

They returned to the intrusive object and looked down on it again, awaiting perhaps an explanation for its presence.

'Come on, Jon. It's late. Let's go to bed, and we'll think about this in the morning.'

'Yes, I am tired, and we're safe in here,' said Jonathan, sliding the safety latch across the door. 'I'm sure there's a simple explanation.'

But they couldn't come up with one the next day.

'Let's try to think about this logically,' Robert suggested. 'Nothing's been stolen, and nothing's been damaged. The only thing that's different is that we now have a peacock feather. You do understand the significance of that, don't you, Jon?'

'Oh God, yes. It hadn't occurred to me before, but now you mention it ... Someone knows about us, Rob. Someone knows what we are! Oh, God.'

'Now, don't get worked up over this, Jon. We must stay focused. It must be a message. A warning, maybe? But from whom? None of our friends would leave us with the feather; there is no need, and even if this had something to do with any of them, they don't have keys to the flat. So, how did someone get in?'

They looked at the Yale lock on the door, and, like everything else, it appeared normal. Robert checked the mechanism, and it worked as it should.

'Whoever got in must have done so by manipulating the lock, somehow, not to mention the front door to the building. I wonder if Jeff and Brenda across the hall know anything. I'll ask them later when we get back from the shop.'

'Rossi?' Jonathan opined. 'First, the card in the shop door, now this. I'd like us to have the locks here changed, Rob. Can we do that, please?'

'Yes, of course. I'll let the landlord's agent know. It'll be okay, I'm quite sure. I don't know about Rossi, though.'

'Thank you.'

'I don't think there's anything else we can do right now, so let's get off to the shop.'

The rain was an annoyance as they squeezed under the one umbrella heading for the station. Saturday mornings were usually fun in the shop, with quite a few customers milling around, but Robert wasn't feeling particularly enthralled with being there today. 'Perhaps the rain would be a deterrent.'

However, he did telephone the landlord's agent to let him know he wanted to change the lock on his front door because of a break-in and was given permission, but it was to be his cost.

Putting down the telephone, he gave the news to Jonathan, who seemed relieved.

'I feel a bit happier now,' he said. 'Right, I have to drop off the Trollope to Julian around the corner, so I'll do that now and pick up a couple of cakes on the way back to have with our morning tea. Yes?'

A few moments after Jonathan had set off on his errand with his umbrella, three figures gathered at the shop's entrance, seemingly sheltering from the rain as the sky darkened, threatening even heavier downpours.

Looking out at their now-almost silhouetted shapes, Robert noticed one of the three was pointing into the shop while one other pushed open the door. They were young, barely out of their teens. They sauntered up to where Robert stood by the desk, their faces contorted in a snarl that sent a shiver down Robert's spine. One of them, the one who had been doing the pointing, was taller and broader than the others. He moved close to Robert.

'All right, fucker,' he sneered, 'hand over the cash.'

'What?' was Robert's immediate response.

'You 'eard. The cash. Now, and be quick abou' it.'

Robert blinked, His mind struggling to process the scene. 'Cash?' he stammered, his voice uncharacteristically high-pitched. 'I ...I don't understand.'

The sneer deepened. 'Don't be a fuckin' prat. You got money here, right? We know you do.'

Panic gnawed at the edges of Robert's consciousness. Violence had no place in his bookshop, a haven of worn spines and whispered stories. He tried reasoning. 'Look, there's been a misunderstanding. I don't keep large sums on hand. Surely ...'

The leader grabbed Robert's jacket lapels and pulled him towards him, his movement surprisingly swift. At the same time, a stack of eighteenth-century novels was being hurled to the floor, erupting in a flurry of forgotten tales. A pang of horror stabbed at Robert as he then watched a first-edition Dickens tumble to the floor, its leather cover scuffed.

'Oops!'

Another of the thugs, with a mop of greasy hair, kicked over a display of travel books, their glossy pages scattering like startled birds. A cold fury, a stranger in his usual calm demeanour, began to simmer in Robert. These weren't customers; they were vandals, defiling the very essence of his shop.

But the fury was quickly doused by another, colder emotion – fear. The hulking figure brandished a flick knife, its glint catching the dim light. The unspoken threat hung heavy in the air – compliance or bloodshed.

'The till,' the thug snarled, gesturing with the knife. Robert's fingers trembled as he opened the drawer. The week's takings stared back at him. He hadn't had a chance to take them to the bank yet.

He scooped it up, his heart a lead weight in his chest. 'Here,' he croaked, pushing the cash towards them. 'That's all there is. Please. Just leave.'

The youth snatched the money, a triumphant smirk twisting his lips. The others, emboldened, pocketed a number of books, not for any intellectual purpose but just because they could. With a final sneer at Robert, they turned and left, their laughter echoing through the ravaged shop as thy ran out into the wet Court.

Robert sank onto a stool, the rain outside a mocking counterpoint to the storm within. His haven was violated, and his peace shattered. He surveyed the damage – the fallen books, like wounded soldiers, seemed to accuse him of his helplessness.

Tears welled up in his eyes, blurring the once-familiar spines. A single thought echoed in his mind – a desperate hope for a world where stories weren't just vessels of imagination but shields against the ugliness that lurked in the shadows.

It was to this devastation that Jonathan and his cakes arrived.

Chapter Ten

It took all morning to get the shop back to normal. Robert had done his best to attend to visitors while doing so but couldn't summon up much enthusiasm. For the first time ever, he considered customers an intrusion on what he had to do, and reluctantly, he had turned the sign on the glass door to 'Closed' to deal with the chaos. Jonathan was a wreck.

Robert had watched him come through the door and take in the scene in absolute horror. He continued to watch as Jonathan's legs had given way. The world around Jonathan seemingly dissolving into nothingness.

As he went down, the box of cream cakes catapulted into the mess and confusion. Robert scrambled quickly to Jonathan's side, just in time to catch the crumbling body in his arms. A low moan escaped Jonathan's lips; his eyes became glassy and unfocused.

It was then that a wave of nausea hit Robert, a dry heave that did nothing to expel the contents of his stomach and almost made him lose his balance, too. But he got his partner to the back of the shop and lowered onto one of the stools. Relief came over him as he helped Jonathan slump forward, his head resting on his knees. His breaths came in shallow gasps, pitiful wheezing accentuating the silence falling over the room.

With tears welling up in his eyes, Jonathan thrust his head forward into Robert's stomach and cried. Robert held him.

It was heartbreaking for Robert to hear his loved one in such distress. He knew Jonathan didn't have the strongest constitution and was prone to feelings of mild hysteria – 'it's the vapours, darling' – but there was something particularly abject about him right now.

Jonathan began slowly to resume his equilibrium between sobs and gasps for air. 'What in God's name has happened, Robbie?'

'We've been turned over, heart. Robbed. I'll tell you more shortly, but I must get this place tidied up and back into some sense of normality. All these books, strewn about and damaged. I have to look after them. You sit there quietly and get your strength back. Do you want a cup of tea?'

'No,' Jonathan replied in his best attempt at stoicism, 'I'll come and help.'

'Are you sure? Please don't do too much; do what you feel capable of and stop if you begin to feel unwell. All right?'

'All right, I promise.'

'And when we're done, I'll get you home.'

'That will be nice. Thank you.'

So, they set about placing the books and racks back in their designated spots. The hurt and damaged books were taken to the counter near the back of the shop to be assessed and dressed wherever possible. However, they knew that some were too damaged to restore, and they would have to have their own sad ceremony later.

'The bastards took some books away with them, too. I don't know which ones yet, so we'll have to do an inventory to find out.'

'Oh, God, Robbie. This is awful.'

The effects of the last two incidents on Jonathan over the following days were startling. A grey filter had settled over his usual vibrant personality. The man who used to laugh with ease and light up a room now seemed to carry the world's weight on his shoulders. As his loving partner, Robert couldn't help but notice the changes.

A strained smile that never quite reached his eyes had replaced his spontaneity. Once filled with animated discussions about art exhibits and book acquisitions, conversations were now punctuated by long, thoughtful silences. Usually sparkling with mischief, his eyes seemed forever shadowed, a dull ache lurking beneath their surface.

Sleep had become a luxury Jonathan could no longer afford. Robert would find him late at night, out of bed, sitting at the table staring into a void, the furrow in his brow speaking volumes.

His appetite, once a testament to his love of good food, had dwindled. Meals, which used to be a chance to catch up and share stories, felt more like a chore. He'd pick at his food, pushing it around his plate with a distracted air as if his mind was elsewhere.

Robert longed to reach out, to offer a listening ear and a supportive shoulder. But Jonathan, usually an open book, had erected walls around himself. He brushed off gentle inquiries, deflecting any attempt to delve deeper. It was like witnessing a vibrant flower wilt in the face of an unrelenting drought.

The worry gnawed at Robert. He knew pushing him wouldn't help yet seeing him like this was agonising. All he could do was be there for him, a silent anchor in the storm he was weathering. Hopefully, when the sun did break through the clouds, he'd know he was there, ready to listen and offer whatever support he needed.

Robert left Jonathan at home during these troubling times, though he wasn't sure whether isolation was the correct thing for him. He had little choice, though.

While Jonathan succumbed to his ennui, Robert tried to work things out about how to manage these alarming incidents. The card in the door, the peacock feather, and the latest, the violence and robbery in the shop were all related, he felt, and that led him to the obvious conclusion that it was Rossi's doing. Yet he hadn't been seen for over a month. Even so, he felt it must be him.

And what of his own emotions right now? The death of Elsie Hatton and the card in the door had confused him. Were the two things related or coincidental? In isolation, it seemed improbable that they were connected, but now perhaps not. Then, the peacock feather in the flat had alarmed him. Someone knew the significance to the queer community of that feather – the symbol of recognition of like souls and had gained access to their home. Their home, where the sketchbook was. The feather meant someone knew about Jonathan and himself, knew of their homosexuality, and that could be dangerous.

And the attack on him in the shop. That had given him serious cause for concern. If all this was Rossi's doing, he wasn't fooling about. Did the sketchbook mean that much to him he would stoop to such awful behaviour? Of course, it did. After all, Robert knew, it meant so, so much to himself.

He thought once more about Rossi's claim to it, and the more he considered it, the more convinced he was that his right to it was spurious and absurd. *Family heirloom, indeed!* But one thing he felt was for sure: Rossi was determined to get it if he could. 'Well, that's something I will not let happen,' he voiced aloud.

It was the next day that Robert experienced further dismay. His heart pounded as he shivered in a Charing Cross Road shop doorway, out of the relentless driving rain. People plunged along the thoroughfare in front of him, their hurried steps muffled by the crackling rain. He peered out at a sea of umbrellas and raincoats trudging to who knew where; their eyes not deviating from the pavement just a couple of feet ahead of them. Passing buses, their wheels churning through puddles, sent arcs of water splashing up, drenching trouser hems and skirts. Shop windows, aglow even at this early hour, offered refuge from the cold. Their neon signs flickering, casting a cold illumination on the wet pavement. It was a real wintry London morning, yet the city still buzzed with a determined energy.

Robert's breath caught in his throat as he squinted at the pair coming towards where he sheltered.

Rossi. The name echoed in his mind like a curse. There he was, unmistakable in his impeccably tailored overcoat, with a woman sharing his umbrella. She clung to Rossi's arm; her crimson lips curved in a wicked smile. Had Robert known that the woman was Sarah Mulholland, he would have gone quite some way to understand what had been happening to Jonathan and himself over the last few weeks.

The notorious gang leader had a reputation that sent shivers through London's underworld. Stories of her ruthlessness – the way she silenced rivals with a single glance – were legendary. It was said that even the Richardsons and Krays gave her grudging respect.

As they neared where Robert stood, he saw Rossi look up and his eyes lock onto his in recognition. A threat hung heavy in the air. The man had promised vengeance after their last meeting. Robert had thought it mere bluster, but now he wondered. Was Rossi here to settle the score? To remind Robert that debts in their world were never fully paid.

As they passed by, Rossi's lips curved into a chilling smile. Robert's legs trembled, but he forced himself to hold his ground. He would not cower. The Italian leaned closer into the woman and whispered something in her ear while still looking in Robert's direction. She looked sharply to where Rossi had indicated and laughed.

He watched them pass by and into the crowd, wondering when he would see Rossi again.

He turned up the collar of his raincoat. 'If Rossi has returned,' he thought, 'then things were likely to come to a head.' He had no idea, however, just what Rossi had in store or how far he would go in his quest to acquire the sketchbook. He could only wait for the next thing to happen.

Rossi and Sarah Mulholland walked on until they reached the café Robert had been going to. There, they entered the warmth from the wet and cold street.

'I do not like your English weather.' Rossi announced as he opened the door and looked for a table. 'I do not intend to stay here longer than necessary.'

'There's a table over there.' Sarah said, pointing, 'You get it, and I'll order coffee for us. Nespresso?'

'It is here, in London? Then, yes, thank you, Sarah.'

Rossi sat down at a Formica-topped table in one of the four chairs and moved the sugar shaker to one side. The café was quite busy, with lots of wet coats and umbrellas humming and humidifying around him. Sarah joined him a few moments later. Rain continued to fall, streaking the window outside and steaming it inside. She sat down opposite him.

'Shouldn't be too long. The waitress'll bring 'em over when they're ready.' The hiss, gurgle and swish of the espresso machine continued its seemingly unending percolation over the café's atmosphere. She tapped her crimson nails on the tabletop. Rossi sat quietly but no less impatient.

'Robert Ferngrove,' Rossi murmured, 'is a man with a weakness that I intend to exploit. With your help, of course.' He said, grinning.

Sarah leaned in, her tailored raincoat brushing against the wooden back of her chair. 'I've been putting the frighteners on Ferngrove over the last few days, as you wanted. What is it that you're actually after?'

Rossi explained about the sketchbook and how it belonged to him, not Ferngrove.

'Is it valuable?'

'Yes, but it is worth more than money to me. It is part of my heritage. I must have it.'

At the mention of money, he could sense that Sarah Mulholland was now more interested in assisting him than ever. He could almost smell her desire. 'So, how do we get this book? Is it at any of the places my boys have visited already?'

'I don't know where it is. I do know that both Ferngrove and his 'partner' …', he curled his lip at the mere suggestion of the disgusting association, 'are scared thanks to you and could be ready to give me the book.'

The waitress arrived and put their cups in front of them. Rossi looked down at the thin beverage in front of him. He hesitatingly took a sip and recoiled in distaste. 'What is this thing? An espresso should have a rich, velvety body. It should be smooth and creamy, not this thin dishwater.'

'I don't think it's too bad,' Sarah said, tracing the rim of her cup. 'It's new in England.'

He pushed his cup aside. 'We will get at Ferngrove through his relationship with Spencer. He won't risk the scandal. He will comply with my demands.' Rossi's gaze shifted to the window. 'Spencer is the way. He is Ferngrove's Achilles heel. We will use him. In fact, we will use anyone he is close to, perhaps his parents and, especially, his sister, Joanna. Yes.' The last word rolled slowly off his tongue.

He had grown rather fond of Joanna Ferngrove, perhaps more than he had for any other woman. He could see a relationship developing with her and he liked the thought. But. And it was a big 'but', the need to have the sketchbook was greater and he realised he was prepared to sacrifice her on the altar of desire.

Satisfied, Andrea raised his cup and sipped, forgetting how awful he found it initially. He didn't alter his opinion.

And so, amidst the rain-slicked streets of Charing Cross Road, Andrea Rossi and Sarah Mulholland forged their pact - a dangerous alliance fuelled by greed, desire, and the promise of a rare book that held the power to unravel lives. It would begin with Sarah paying a visit to Ferngrove's shop.

'Andy, my boy, keep the payments coming, and I'll do anything for ya!'

Robert, meanwhile, had hurried along the sodden footpath past the café and back towards the shop. All desire for that café's welcoming hot espresso extinguished.

He had just put his soaking-wet raincoat on a coat hanger at the back of the shop when he heard someone enter. He was becoming almost fearful of the tinkling doorbell now but beamed when he saw that the person coming toward him was a good friend.

Simon Williams, whom he had met last year through connections with Lord Henderson, was 27 years old, married to Lisa, and had gorgeous twins, David and

Angela. He was a freelance journalist with a keen interest in social matters. He was straight.

'Simon! So good to see you again. How's life treating you?' They shook hands.

'Very well, thanks, Robert. And you?'

'Not too bad. You here to buy some books?'

'Not today, I'm afraid, but I need your help. I'd like you to have a look at a draft of an article I've written. I'd like to know if I have written it with the right amount of empathy and that it's slanted to the correct degree. You know that I am aware of your and Jonathan's sexual orientation and have no problems with it. Oh God, I sound condescending. I don't mean to.'

'No, no, that's all right, Simon, you're not.'

'Can we sit down somewhere and go through it? Maybe at the café in Charing Cross Road when the rain eases off?'

There was hesitation in Robert's voice when he agreed.

'Oh look, if you aren't happy to do this …'

'No, sorry, Simon, it's fine. There was someone in that café that I don't want to meet. Can we leave it until later in the day?'

'Of course, though, you should see what a normal day in the life of Simon Williams, London-based freelance journalist, is like. I'll show you a snippet of my diary memoir, too.'

'That's a deal,' Robert laughs. 'Come back at around four? Unless I'm swamped, I'll close up, and then we'll go for that coffee.'

'Done. See you then.'

Robert's concern was that he may have to face Rossi during the day and was gearing himself up for it all day. But four o'clock came. The heavy rain had eased to a steady drizzle. Rossi hadn't appeared. Simon was bang on time.

He closed up the shop, and the two men headed off for the café.

Chapter Eleven

'Thanks for helping me with this, Robert. I need a little, how shall I say it, 'expert' help on an article I'm looking to get published soon. Fleet Street won't touch it, as they're pushing their own barrow in quite the opposite direction.'

'Of course, if I can. What is it?'

'Peter offered to help but felt you and Jonathan were better suited for the task. I think he was concerned about any negative publicity.'

'Oh. And we're not?' Robert said mockingly.

'No. No, I didn't mean ...'

'That's alright Simon. Only joking. Jonathan's not here at the moment but what is it you want from us?'

'Would you have a look at this for me and tell me what you think.' He fished the article out of his satchel. Robert took it from him while Simon went to order their espresso coffees and began to read.

Draft of Article:

A clandestine world unfolds in the murky corners of 1961 London, where fog clings to cobblestone streets and secrets are whispered through the cracks. For homosexual men, life is a delicate dance between survival and desire, arrest and affection – a tightrope stretched across the abyss of danger and hope.

In 1885, the Criminal Amendment Act – the law used to prosecute Oscar Wilde in 1895 – passed through Parliament. It raised the age of sexual consent from 13 to 16 for heterosexual persons, thereby outlawing child prostitution. The law also stated in section 11 that 'any male person who, in public or private, commits any act of gross indecency with another male person shall be guilty of a misdemeanour, and being convicted thereof shall be liable at the discretion of the court to be imprisoned for any term not exceeding two years, with or without hard labour.'

That law today still casts its shadow over every stolen glance, every furtive but caring touch. Men who love men risk imprisonment, their lives forever altered by a society that deems their affections abhorrent. Merely loving the wrong person could make you a criminal. Smiling in the park could lead to arrest, and being in the wrong address book could result in a prison sentence. The British Law Society defines the homosexual, or queer, as a potent challenge to normative domesticity: an attack on marriage, a barrier to demographic stability, and a threat to the nation's youth. This is an evil, it claims, that the state will not tolerate.

Homosexuality is illegal, and hundreds of thousands of men fear being picked up by zealous police wanting easy convictions, often for doing nothing more than looking different. Men must meet in hidden and risky spaces unless they are wealthy and can meet and socialise more freely at private parties and clubs; public parks like Hampstead Heath, Hyde Park, and Clapham Common, where discreet signals and coded language identify them. At underground bars and clubs, hidden from public view and operating with the constant threat of police raids. Finding these places often relied on word-of-mouth within the close-knit community.

Then there are the public toilets, which, because of a lack of safer spaces, must be a meeting place for many and where the possibility of arrest by undercover police is high.

This was the scene where John Simpson found himself in February this year. John glanced nervously around in the dimly lit public toilet off the Chelsea Embankment. The air was thick with anticipation and secrecy. He was being forced to find solace in clandestine encounters such as these. He was a middle-aged accountant who lived a double life. By day, he balanced ledgers and navigated the mundane routines of a respectable existence. But at night, he ventured into the city's hidden corners –the discreetly lit pubs, the furtive alleyways –where forbidden love awaited.

The porcelain tiles were chipped, and the walls were stained with years of furtive liaisons. John adjusted his tie, his heart racing. He had met James here, a fellow man seeking forbidden pleasure. Their eyes had locked, and desire had ignited –an unspoken understanding transcending societal norms.

As John leaned against the graffiti-covered stall, he heard footsteps approaching. Panic surged through him. Was it the police? Did someone tip them off? He had heard stories of men being arrested for 'cottaging' – the euphemism for cruising public toilets in search of illicit connections.

The door creaked open, revealing a burly officer with a stern expression. John's breath caught. The officer's gaze bore into him; suspicion etched on his face. John's mind raced – his life and reputation all hanging in the balance.

'Caught in the act, aren't we?' The officer's voice dripped with disdain. 'Soliciting for immoral purposes.'

John's heart pounded. He had no defence, no alibi. James had vanished, leaving him exposed. The officer's grip tightened as he led John out of the toilet into the unforgiving London streets.

The police station smelled of dampness and bureaucracy. John sat on a hard wooden bench, his palms clammy. The cell door clanged shut, sealing his fate. The charge: gross indecency. The punishment: imprisonment.

His secret behaviour had gnawed at John's soul. He yearned for acceptance of what he was, but the world outside was unyielding. The newspapers mocked 'deviants,' the police prowled, and whispers of arrests circulated like poison.

His friends had suspected nothing. They saw a bachelor, a man devoted to his work. They didn't know about the nights he wept into his pillow, torn between love and duty. He realised now that they would know.

The scene described is like so many others that have come before the courts, but it isn't just the illegal aspect of homosexual activity that is of concern. That he has sexual urges brought on by other men means he has a medical condition that requires treatment, so the government believes.

One only has to consider the treatment meted out in the 1950s to Alan Turing, a gifted mathematician whose work at Bletchley Park during the Second World War helped break the Enigma machine codes. Instead of treating him as a national hero, they condemned him as a homosexual upon discovering his love for another man. Doctors subjected him to medical rectification or chemical castration.

So why this horrific aversion? Besides religious reasons, the 1950s saw a genuine fear of communism spreading throughout Europe; therefore, people considered non-conformist behaviour subversive and sought to eliminate it. This fear persists to this day.

That a male can be born a homosexual is an anathema to today's standards of 'normality'. It is widely thought that a boy chooses to become queer or, more probably, is induced into becoming queer by older men. The doctrine of normality thus implies that he can be cured. The most common treatment involves behavioural aversion therapy, where they attach electrodes to the patient's wrist or lower leg and administer electric shocks while the patient looks at photographs of men and women in various stages of undress.

This aims to encourage avoidance of the shock by moving to photographs of the opposite sex. It is hoped that arousal to same-sex photographs will reduce, while relief arising from shock avoidance will increase interest in opposite-sex images.

Some patients have reported undergoing a detailed examination before treatment, with others being assessed more perfunctorily. Patients are required to recline on a bed or sit in a chair in a darkened room, alone or with a professional behind a screen. Each treatment lasts about 30 minutes, then some participants receive portable electric shock boxes to use at home while they induce sexual fantasies. Patients continue to attend a hospital as outpatients for weeks and, in some instances, up to two years.

It's time to implement the 1957 Wolfenden Report's main recommendation – decriminalising private, consensual homosexual acts between adults – thus significantly altering our views on sexuality and individual liberties.

Let the Report bring about widespread conversation about sexuality and morality. Let it bring about reform. This is 1961, after all, not 1855.

'Heavens, Simon, that's pretty forthright stuff. Will you be able to get it published?'

'Good question, Rob. It's quite controversial – which is what I want – and some newspapers and journals may have issues running it, but the more contemporary publications, I am sure, will find it of value. But is it okay? Does it resonate with you?'

'Yes, it certainly does. It's about time someone revealed the truth. Good luck with it. And please let me know which publications are going to carry it. Now, what's this memoir thing you were talking about?'

Simon retrieved the article from Robert and stored it away in his satchel before producing a second piece of work, which he placed in front of his friend.

'This is just a snippet from a book I'm creating. It comprises my daily routine over a period of, I think, one month, depending on whether it is too samey. It's a kind of educational journal for prospective journalists, stripping away the supposed glamour of the profession and showing it as it is in reality.'

'I'm not sure yet whether to keep it in this format or make it more narrative. I think this works best, though. Have a look and see what you think. It'll need a bit of beefing out.'

Robert read:

Day 12 in the life of Simon Williams, Journalist.:

Morning:

- **7:00 AM**: Simon wakes up in his modest Pimlico flat. The kitchenette's percolator fills the room with the faint scent of coffee.
- **7:30 AM**: After a quick shower, he kisses his wife, Lisa, and David and Angela, their lovely but unexpected twins, now two years old – bright-eyed and eager for the day –before heading out.

- **8:00 AM**: Simon hops on his Vespa scooter, navigating the bustling London streets. His destination: Shared office space in Soho.

At the office

- **8:30 AM**: Arriving at his cluttered desk, Simon sifts through stacks of newspapers. He scans headlines, underlining critical points for his articles.
- **9:00 AM**: The room buzzes with activity. Simon huddles with colleagues, discussing the latest stories –the Cold War tensions, the space race, and, of particular interest to him, the developing civil rights movement in both the USA and Britain.
- **10:00 AM**: He types a piece for his current article and writes notes on other possible, saleable articles
- **11:00 AM**: Simon dashes to the canteen for a quick bacon sandwich. He chats with fellow journalists, sharing anecdotes and insider gossip.
- **11:30 AM**: Back at his desk, he continues to type on his manual typewriter, crafting a feature article on the arrest of over 1,300 protesters in Trafalgar Square during a CND rally. He remembers to insert carbon paper this time.

Lunchtime:

- **1:00 PM**: Simon joins a press conference at Westminster. The Prime Minister's speech echoes in his mind as he scribbles notes.
- **2:00 PM**: Lunch with a source –a cabinet minister who spills secrets over fish and chips. Simon's notebook fills with cryptic phrases: 'cabinet minister', 'scandal', 'sex'.

Afternoon:

- **3:00 PM:** He pops along to the British Library to research the effects of gambling on families after the Betting and Gaming Act of 1960 legalised betting shops earlier that year.
- **4:30 PM**: Simon returns to his office to collect his things and then heads home. It is his turn to babysit while Lisa goes to her badminton classes.

Evening:

- **7:00 PM**: With the kids fed and in bed and the flat to himself, Simon cooks a meal for when Lisa returns. A relaxing scotch in hand. He will look at his library notes later before bed.

As usual, a blend of adrenaline, curiosity, and dedication – a dance between headlines and heartbeats.

'Again, Simon, fascinating. Unique, I feel, though you may have only a limited market for it as a book.'

'You could well be right about that, but I'm hopeful about it.'

Robert handed the piece back.

'It would be fantastic if we could catch up again. I would offer to have you both over to our place, but it's a bit small, and with two small kids, it's not conducive...'

'No, that's fine. I'd love for us to catch up too. Why don't you and Lisa come over to our place? Are you okay with babysitters?'

'No problems at all. And, yes, we'd love to. I'll check with Lisa, and we'll arrange a date.'

With that, Simon swept out of the café and Robert headed off to the tube station.

Chapter Twelve

Sarah Mulholland lacked a good education. She attended a charity school in Stepney, in the East end of London, and at fourteen in 1933, finished her schooling, for what it was, and left. She may not have been an outstanding pupil, but she was no fool.

Sarah soon realised that, after her dad had walked out of the rented two-bedroom terraced home in Miller Street, she had the gift of being able to attract people to her – people who seemed happy to either do things for her or give her things. She inherited these skills from her mother, through a sort of osmosis, who used them to attract 'men friends', as she called the regular visits to their house.

Sarah was well aware of her good looks and sensuousness that echoed her mother's charms from an early age. It was, in fact, one of her mother's men friends that made her realise she had something that gave her some sort of power. She had seen how the men had drooled over and pawed her mother and how they were happy to bring her presents in response to her giving them her time. When the first of the men to divert his attention to the then thirteen-year-old attempted to place his hand on her thigh as they sat on the lounge waiting for Mother to return from upstairs, Sarah told him it would cost him a tanner to do that and that further feelings would increase the charge. Either pay up or her mother would learn of what he'd been up to with a 'mere schoolgirl'.

Having realised how she could manipulate one man to give her money, Sarah then set about enticing others of her mother's male visitors, offering them a look or a feel of her growing breasts or a fiddle inside her drawers for an appropriate fee. Even when any of the men declined her offers, Sarah would still threaten to tell her mother that they had ill-treated her daughter unless, of course, they paid her not to.

This business became quite lucrative, and soon she was extending her opportunities into the street, threatening to report respectable-looking men to the police for violating her person.

After leaving school, her business evolved as she was able to devote more time to her pursuits: theft, extortion, errand-running, and, ultimately, prostitution. However, the errand running was the beginning of her business empire. She would recruit younger boys to do the legwork, paying them a small fee and leaving her a profit, which she ploughed back into her operations.

The prostitution side of the business was next to take off. Demand for such services was rife, but her 'supply' was insufficient. She recruited some of her old school pals who were desperate to avoid the local factory or the poor house. Her standards of hygiene and behavioural demands soon began attracting workers in addition to clientele. It became clear to Sarah that street prostitution was dangerous for her girls, so she began looking for suitable premises. When she acquired a number of 'hostels', her career flourished. She was twenty-one.

She branched out into the protection industry, collecting her rents from bookkeepers, publicans, and shopkeepers with the aid of several non-discerning male collectors. Wartime did not hinder Sarah's business development, and by the time hostilities ended, she occupied a most respectable apartment in Belgravia. Her now utterly respectable business had evolved into an escort agency with clients that could afford her high-quality girls' rates.

When she had the time – and she always seemed to find it – she played at illegal casinos, usually at the exclusive Fitzroy Club. There, she would mix with aristocracy, crooks, and dinner-jacketed achievers in the club's upper room, sited between the first and second floors, where cigar smoke and iced drinks intertwined with scantily clad girls (hers) and fat gambling chips.

When she met Andrea Rossi for the first time at the club, she was thirty-six years old, though from her appearance, she looked nowhere near that age, closer to Rossi's twenty-six. She saw in the young man a person of similar attitude to herself: on the outside, he was attractive, charming, and alluring, while she discerned he was self-absorbed, single-minded and potentially wilful. He naturally appealed to her.

Sarah learned from the Italian that he, like her, had never married, overlooked in their pursuits of their own material happiness. Occasionally, she regretted not being in love, but mostly, she considered it a vulnerability and a hindrance to her worldly desires.

Rossi had recruited her to find out about the activities of a particular wealthy businessman who frequented the club. He had heard that this chairman of a once-prosperous industrial concern in England and Italy had used company funds to support his gambling habit and was, therefore, exposed to approaches from a man such as Rossi. And that proved to be the case. Rossi bought the business = which he on sold for a considerable profit - paid Sarah handsomely for her assistance, and the former chairman was never seen again at the club.

Therefore, she was delighted to receive his letter some five years later, advising that he was returning to London to carry out further business and would welcome seeing her again at his Savoy Hotel. He received her positive reply in time.

The woman that Robert had seen yesterday with Rossi in the rain approached him as he stood behind the shop's counter. With her was the thug that had stolen his money last Saturday. His heart rate shot up alarmingly.

'Good morning. You are Mr Ferngrove, I believe,' the woman announced calmly and quietly in an improved east-end accent, then awaited his response.

'Erm, yes, that's right.'

'You have met my colleague here, of course.'

Robert looked from the woman to the cocky-looking thug. 'I have,' he said, returning his gaze to her.

'My name is Sarah Mulholland. I run several very successful businesses here in London, and am a friend of Mr Andrea Rossi, someone I know you are familiar with. Isn't that so, Mr Ferngrove?'

As much as his fear would allow, Robert tried to take in this woman and understand her role in this horror story. 'Yes, I know Rossi.' His voice conveyed the dryness in his throat. He could also feel a trickle of sweat between his shoulder blades and his hands' clamminess. 'What do you want?'

'All in good time. You have some pretty books here.' She gesticulated around the shop. Her colleague, the thug, grinned. Robert worried the thug would inflict more damage on his beloved stock, raising his anxiety levels. 'Is the business profitable?'

'It's all right.'

'You run it with a partner, is that right?'

'Yes.'

'And where is he?'

'He's not in the shop today.'

'No, he isn't, is he?'

That comment worried Robert even more. Had she or Rossi got to Jonathan? Hurt him?

'And you have some valuable books here. Is that right?'

'Yes, some.'

'Show me one.'

Robert pointed to a limited-edition Dickens.

'Interesting. What makes it valuable?'

Robert laboured in his breathing as he attempted to explain about limited prints and first editions, and he feared for the book's well-being.

She sauntered over to where Robert had pointed and looked at the spine of the book. 'Does it have pictures?'

'Pictures?'

'Yes. Pictures.'

'Well, no, not that one.'

'But you do have books with pictures.' It was a statement, not a question.

'Art books, you mean. We have some, but the shop along the way there has …'

'I'm not interested in other shops' books. I want to know about your art books. Or, should I say, to be more accurate, one particular art book that belongs to my friend, Mr Rossi.'

So, there it is, thought Robert. We get to the heart of the matter at last. But he wondered how defiant he could be towards this woman.

'Mrs Mulholland ...'

'Miss Mulholland.'

'Oh, sorry. I'm afraid, Miss Mulholland, that I have nothing belonging to Mr Rossi.'

'That is not what I've been told, Mr Bookseller. I've been told that you do. Are you saying that either Mr Rossi or, heaven forbid, I am lying?' The thug's presence loomed more menacingly.

'No, I didn't say that, only that Mr Rossi is mistaken.'

'Mistaken? He doesn't think so. He has asked me to come here today to let you know that, without fail, he will get the book from you. He has certain knowledge about you and Mr Spencer that he will use unless you comply with his demands.'

Robert wanted desperately to be brave and tell her to let Rossi know what he could do with his so-called demands, but the reality was he couldn't say that. He could, however, internalise the strength.

'Please inform Mr Rossi that he must do what he thinks he can. The sketchbook is mine, and nothing will make me give it up.'

'Even if it means that your parents and your sister will become involved?'

'What do you mean?'

'Accidents happen to people every day, and when a person is in a foreign country on her own, well, who knows what difficulties they could get into.'

'He wouldn't hurt Joanna. Not after all he has done for her. Would he?'

'Possibly. Possibly not. It depends on how much he wants that book and how much you are determined to hang onto it. Oh, and he asked me to tell you that not only is homosexuality a crime, but the social disgrace of being identified as one would be horrendous. He might be driven to expose your situation to the world.'

This was what Robert was fearing. Blackmail. He wasn't at all sure how to deal with this. Yet.

'I'll have to talk this over with my partner.'

'Naturally. But Mr Rossi's patience is wearing thin. He will see you at his hotel the day after tomorrow. Sunday morning, at eleven. You should bring your answer and the book.'

With that, Sarah Mulholland turned and headed for the door, her lapdog thug trailing behind her. As she opened it, she looked behind her at Robert and smiled. 'Sunday at eleven.' And she was gone.

Alone again in his shop, Robert could feel himself trembling; the adrenaline rush from the confrontation had left him with this shaking sensation. He could feel a tightness in his chest as the anxiety and tension belatedly took hold.

Emotionally, Robert felt numbness and disorientation. It took several moments for this to dissipate, and he struggled to fully process what had just happened. When he did, he was left with an initial feeling of disbelief, which then turned to anger and resentment toward this woman, first of all, for bringing this nastiness into their shop, and then Andrea Rossi, for being the cause of it all.

The physical and mental turmoil occurred so quickly that Robert couldn't grasp just what he was feeling. Hurt now invaded his emotional state, followed rapidly by a strong sense of insecurity.

The customer who entered the shop at that moment did a great deal to force Robert to 'get a grip' and manage his circumstances and his environment. After the visitor had completed his purchase, Robert sat at the back of the shop, calmness returning to him, and reflected on all that had happened.

He could now think more clearly but couldn't determine his next course of action. Yes, he thought, I will meet with Rossi on Sunday. Not Jonathan and not the sketchbook. I won't part with it. What will I do if he goes ahead with his threat? I don't know. Should I tell Jonathan? He has a right to know. It might cause further pain for him. Yes. What about Joanna? Mum and Dad? Should I tell them, in case? I don't know. I just don't know.

The day dragged on for Robert. His mind was not as focused on his customers as it should have been, but at least he kept busy for most of the time and didn't fret over the looming problems with Rossi. For good or for bad, Robert decided against telling Jonathan about the day's events. His mental state was just about recovered from the last incident, he concluded, so adding this latest issue would be too harmful for him.

So, Robert closed up at five o'clock and joined the throng, heading home in the dark of the late October afternoon. Office workers, wrapped in overcoats and scarves, their collars turned up against the chill, poured out of buildings and into the bustling thoroughfares around Charing Cross Road. The air was thick with the scent of rain-soaked concrete and petrol fumes from the humming traffic as a legion of people made their way towards Leicester Square tube station.

The crowd moved with a sense of urgency, jostling and hurrying, eager to escape the dreary weather and begin their weekend. Conversations were muted, drowned out by the cacophony of footsteps and the occasional honk of a taxi. Determined expressions adorned faces, eyes focused on the path ahead, each person lost in their own thoughts of warmth and home.

As they descended into the underground station, the atmosphere shifted. The musty warmth of the tube replaced the cold, damp air, and the sound of footsteps echoed off the tiled walls. The throng funnelled through the ticket barriers. Here, the crowd splintered, smaller bodies of people heading towards their respective lines and destinations.

Robert, among the sea of commuters, felt a small sense of relief. Unlike many, his journey was relatively short. He boarded the southbound Northern Line train that stopped at Waterloo, finding a rare empty seat for the eleven-minute trip. He glanced around at his fellow passengers. Some passengers engrossed themselves in their newspapers, while others stared blankly at the advertisements lining the walls. The rhythmic clatter of the train was almost soothing, a stark contrast to the chaos and trauma that had occurred above ground.

For Robert, the journey was a brief respite, a moment to unwind before the short walk to the peace of home and Jonathan's now improving company. As the train approached Waterloo, he stood up, ready to face the last leg of his journey home. The doors opened, and he stepped out onto the platform, along with the long-distance commuters headed for the mainline station that would take them to places as far away as Woking, Guildford and, in some cases, the south coast and Southampton. He was so glad not to have to face those journeys each day.

As he walked along Waterloo Road, he organised his thoughts on what to tell Jonathan. Satisfied with what he decided to say, he stopped off at the florist shop, as it prepared to close, to buy an end-of-day, slightly wilting bunch of the sweet-smelling pink dianthus.

Chapter Thirteen

'I'm home!' Robert announced, removing his key from the front door lock and entering the flat. The tantalising aroma of something cooking drifted through the room, curling into his nostrils and awakening his senses. It was a rich, savoury scent layered with hints of garlic and herbs, promising a meal that would be nothing short of delicious. His stomach growled in response, a reminder of how long it had been since he ate. The warmth of the kitchen enveloped him, a stark contrast to the damp chill of the late October afternoon outside. The scent seemed to wrap around him, pulling him towards the kitchen where the source of this culinary delight awaited, offering a comforting refuge from the grey of the world beyond the window.

'Hello, heart. How are you?' Robert approached the aproned Jonathan, who turned from the cooktop to welcome him. 'I bought these on the way. A bit tired, I'm afraid, but they're still lovely.' He handed them out to Jonathan, who beamed at seeing both them and him.

'They're just lovely, Rob. Good choice, as always. I'll get a vase. I'm well, thanks.' He gave Robert a kiss on the lips. 'Can't hug, or I'll crush the blooms! How was your day? G and T?'

'I'll get them just as soon as I've put my coat and scarf away and kicked my shoes off.'

Jonathan placed the vase and flowers on the dining table and returned to his kitchen tasks.

Robert re-emerged at the busy scene with the drinks. 'I'll tell you about my day in a jiff. How are you feeling now?'

'Oh, I'm alright. Tell you what, though, I do enjoy being the housewife. Pottering about, making things nice for us. I could get used to it.' He said, smiling.

Did he mean it? Robert wondered. 'Cheers.' They clinked glasses and sipped their drinks. 'We sold the Catullus today,' he announced almost nonchalantly.

'We didn't! My gosh, that's brilliant. To whom? Anyone known?'

'No one we've sold to before. A chap up from Oxford. Reading Classics there, I gather.'

'Well done, you. We'll drink to that.' And they did.

'We had a few people in and made some other sales, so that was good. However, we did have another visitor. A messenger, really.' Robert saw the questioned expression on Jonathan's face. 'From Rossi. He's in London again and wants me to meet him.' The expression turned to one of apprehension.

'Are we going to?'

'It wasn't really an invitation, more a summons. It's on Sunday, and I will go, but I think you'd be better off staying here.'

'I'm not going to argue with you about that, Rob. I don't think my nerves could stand it. Will you be taking the book with you?'

'Absolutely not. I don't want that man coming anywhere near it.'

'Has Rossi actually ever seen it?'

'You know, I don't think he has. Isn't that interesting? He hasn't since it's been with us, and I get the impression he didn't at Guido's shop, or before. So, no.'

'So, he doesn't even know what the book contains?'

'He knows it's an art book that belonged to Turner. That Turner sketched scenes of Venice in it, but more than that, I don't know. I don't think so. You're not suggesting that we could swap it for another?'

'Well …'

'It's an intriguing thought, Jon, but surely we couldn't get away with it, and, anyway, where would we get a substitute?'

'Hmm, good point. Just a thought.' Jonathan said resignedly.

'No. You might have something there. It needs a bit more consideration. Do we have any of Turner's works in the shop? Are there any in the Court?'

'I can't remember seeing any. But, Rob, it would have to be old. Where could we find one of those? And more to the point, how could we afford to buy one?'

'Doesn't seem likely, does it, sadly?'

In bed that night, with Jonathan asleep, Robert lay on his back in the dark, listening to the rain spattering the window and thinking about the Sunday meeting with Rossi. He refused to entertain any thought of handing the sketchbook over to the Italian or, indeed, to anyone, regardless of what they may offer for it. Nothing was going to change his mind about that! He also knew that Jonathan believed he should sell the book and use the money for the future of the business.

But he just doesn't understand what the book means to me. I couldn't give it up. It's mine. I must have it. I've got to get that across to Rossi. He needs to understand what I feel about this. Then perhaps he'll leave us alone. And anyway, why should I even share it, let alone sell it? No one understands the power it has. Everyone will want to take it from me. To exploit it.

A part of him knew this wasn't true. His friends, his family – they cared about him. They'd be happy for him, proud even. But another part, a darker part, whispered insidiously in his ear.

They'll betray you. They'll pretend to care but only want the book for themselves.

He squeezed his eyes shut, trying to drown out the conflicting voices. He felt possessive and secretive.

It's not irrational, he told himself firmly. *It's self-preservation. I have to protect it. It's my responsibility.*

Yet, deep down, he felt a pang of guilt. Was he losing himself to this obsession? Was the sketchbook worth the cost of his peace, his relationships?

'No,' he muttered, shaking his head. 'It's worth it. It has to be.'

With that, Robert rose quietly, went over to the wardrobe, and opened its doors. Kneeling down, he turned the safe's dial to the numbers that would unlock it. He extracted the sketchbook carefully and, rising, took it out of the room and to the dining table, where he laid the book down on the table and switched on a lamp. Sitting almost reverentially in front of his relic, he opened the book to where the first of the two 'special' sketches were. He devoured the scene again with his eyes, and the scene in Venice with Byron and the woman captivated him. Robert touched the page lightly and hovered his fingers over the poet's naked form, his erect penis that she was holding. He, too, touched it and felt an electrifying shiver up his arm and into his soul. It held him there in a timeless, surreal ménage à trois. He was with them, bonded. He was inside the page, the room, the bodies.

'Are you all right, Robert?'

Jonathan's voice broke the spell. He was startled back into his flat in Southwark again tonight, now, flesh and bone.

'Yes, sorry to wake you, Jon. Come on, let's go back to bed.'

He lovingly rubbed Jonathan's cold arm, closed and picked up the book, and turned off the lamp. With the book back inside the safe, they got back into bed.

Jonathan was quickly asleep, though Robert lay awake, torn between the man he used to be and the being he realised he was becoming. With all its allure and mystery, the sketchbook had him ensnared in its embrace, and he wasn't sure he even wanted to be free of it.

Next morning, Jonathan announced he was going to the shop with Robert, and both set off through the annoying drizzle and greyness. It pleased Robert that Jonathan was accompanying him and realised he had missed his presence there the last few days.

Saturday in the shop was enjoyable and passed quickly. That evening, as they prepared their meal, Jonathan returned to their conversation of the night before, but Robert confidently laid aside any thought of trying to trick Rossi about the book. He would simply repeat that it was not for sale. End of story!

After a late breakfast, Robert set off for his meeting with Rossi. As arranged, Robert left the sketchbook at home with Jonathan, who undoubtedly would remain pensive until his return. The rain and drizzle had stopped yesterday afternoon, leaving just the drabness of another late October London day. Robert was thankful for that as he walked the familiar route to Waterloo Station and knew he would be when walking from Charing Cross Station to the Savoy Hotel. He was on time. The lobby's fragrance was its usual blend of eucalyptus and rosemary, giving it a fresh, aromatic, welcoming quality. It gave Robert a little lift from his apprehension.

Reception rang Rossi's room, and two minutes later, a still-nervous Robert Ferngrove was shaking the proffered hand of the poised Andrea Rossi.

'I believe we may have mishandled our last meeting, Mr Ferngrove. Let us hope we can do better this time. You are not with your partner?' Rossi indicated a seating area for Robert to move to. Robert said nothing but sat where shown. 'Would you like some tea? Or coffee? I am having coffee.'

A little tension eased from Robert. 'Yes, thank you. I'll have coffee with you. And, yes, I'm on my own today.'

'Good. See, we have started well.' Rossi paused. 'Mr Ferngrove, I wish to tell you more about my history so you may understand what the sketchbook means to me. The last time we met, I explained in general terms why I consider the book to be mine. No, please, Mr Ferngrove, please remain seated and let me tell you why this is the case. Will you do that, please?'

'It won't do any good. I'm ...'

'Please, Mt Ferngrove. Let me tell it.'

'All right, if you must.'

'Thank you. I was born in Milan, but my mother was Venetian and her, how you say, lineage was from that city, covering many generations. I know this because I have conducted research into these matters, and it has been confirmed to be so. I have documents to show it.'

'One of my ancestors was a Margherita Fornaio. She was born in Venice in 1795 and married Paolo Cogni in 1817. In 1819, she became the poet Lord Byron's lover when he was staying at the Palazzo Mocenigo in Venice. She also met the English artist Turner at the Palazzo when he visited that year. I am led to believe that on his departure from Venice, Mr Turner gave her his sketchbook – the one you presently possess – as a gift. Naturally, she would have treasured the book. She returned to her husband and young son, Francesco, after Byron left her and Venice.

'The sketchbook was hidden away from her husband, who would probably have sold it, until her death. In 1843, two years before Margherita's death, Francesco married and opened a pensione in a Calle close to the Grand Canal in Venice. At his mother's death, Francesco rescued her clothes and other items and stored them in the attic of the pensione. Here they remained, forgotten seemingly, as the business passed to future generations of my family.

'The pensione was closed down during the Second World War, and the building stood empty until 1960 when new tenants, not my family, began clearing everything from the building to enable internal modernisation. The sketchbook, then not in the best of condition seemingly, was found and taken to a second-hand bookseller – your Guido Zampelli – to be disposed of.'

Rossi halted his narrative at that point as the coffees arrived, and each drank a little before he resumed.

'I have visited the pensione and can confirm that the owner found the book and took it to the bookseller. So, you see, Mr Ferngrove, I have a legitimate claim to this book and wish to acquire it from you. I can show you a genealogico, erm, how you say, family tree. I am not an unreasonable man and can be generous in my affairs, as my previous offers to buy the book from you show. I again say to you that the book must come to me.'

'I can see why the sketchbook may mean a lot to you, given that history,' Robert calmly responded. 'But there are a number of inconsistencies that put your lineal ownership in doubt. First, and the most crucial point for me, is that when your family ceased to own the hotel in Venice, the new tenants, who are, as you admit, not related to you, took over all aspects of the business and so became owners of any stock or items that your family may have left.

'Please. Don't interrupt. Second, if the book was considered a valued heirloom, why wasn't it properly cared for?

'Third, you could not identify the book were it to be shown to you, as you have never seen it and have no idea of its contents.

'And fourth – and I'm sure I could think of other reasons – I purchased the book from a legitimate retailer: The bookshop owner that the new hotel owner and, I might emphasise, the new owner of the book, took to him. And that, Mr Rossi, makes me the true owner of the sketchbook. It is not for sale at any price.'

'This is ridiculous, Ferngrove. The book belongs to my family. It is for me to honour that and take it back to Italy. What is it to you? Just another book that you find interesting.'

'It doesn't matter what my reasons are. The book is mine, and it is staying mine.'

There was venom in Rossi's voice as he spoke 'I have warned you before and have shown you I mean business. Things will escalate from here; you can be sure of that. I offer you one more chance to let me buy the book from you.'

'No.'

'Then we have nothing more to say except know that I know about you. I know where you live. I know where your family are, including your sister and your partner's family.'

'You leave them out of this; it has nothing to do with them.'

'Perhaps it hasn't, but it is a way to influence you. And, Mr Ferngrove, I know you are a homosexual. A deviant. I will not hesitate to use that to my advantage. You can be sure of that.

'You can discount nothing. I am a man that gets what he wants by whatever means necessary. You would be wise to consider this.

'Now, I ask you again for the book.'

'Get lost.'

With that, Robert stood and left Rossi. He did have serious concerns about what the Italian might now do, but not enough to dissuade him from his defiance.

Chapter Fourteen

'Well, that went just as I expected,' announced Robert, closing the flat's front door. 'He had nothing new to say, just the usual claim of ownership and threats when I refused to accept his so-called legitimacy over his rights to the sketchbook.'

'Threats? What threats?' Jonathan started to panic again.

'Nothing we haven't heard before, Jon. Nothing to be concerned about.'

'You sure?'

'I'm sure. Now, how about that pasta dish you promised? Then, perhaps, we could pop over to the Anchor this evening and catch up with Gordon and Clive. They're bound to be there. What d'you think?'

'Yes, I'd like that. I haven't seen those two for such a long time, and it'll be nice to get out and have some fun.'

The four men sat in a corner of the lounge bar at the Anchor Tavern. As the other three laughed at some weak pun that Clive had made, Robert, his fingers wrapped around a glass of gin and tonic, looked up pensively at the dark, polished wooden beams above him as they creaked softly, a testament to the pub's age and history. He took a slow sip, the cool liquid a welcome contrast to the warmth radiating from the nearby brick fireplace.

The bar, smelling of cigarette smoke, was dimly lit, with soft, golden light emanating from wall-mounted lanterns and a few hanging chandeliers. It cast a cosy glow over the room, highlighting the worn leather upholstery of the high-backed chairs and the heavy wooden tables scattered throughout. The low ceiling, with its exposed wooden beams, would have added to the intimate atmosphere had Robert been conscious of it.

His gaze wandered over the bar counter, made of dark mahogany with brass fittings that gleamed in the soft light. Behind it, shelves lined with bottles of spirits and a selection of ales on tap stood as a testament to the tavern's well-stocked offerings. He felt a sadness, a heaviness come over him.

Old photographs, paintings, and memorabilia adorned the walls, each piece telling a story of the pub's long connection to the local community. Wooden panelling and exposed brickwork added to the rustic charm, while small, leaded windows with heavy curtains kept the cold at bay.

Robert usually found solace in the pub's many nooks; small, intimate spaces separated by wooden partitions. From his seat, he could see the other patrons, their conversations an indistinct murmur that blended with the crackling of the fire. He watched as a couple by the window laughed softly, their faces illuminated by the flickering light.

Occasionally, Robert's eyes drifted to the small terrace offering a view of the Thames. The river's gentle flow was not visible in the evening dark, but its presence added a sense of calm to the scene. He took another sip of his drink but couldn't capture the peace of mind the pub normally bestowed on him. He had to admit to himself that he was worried about Rossi.

'Don't you think so, Robbie?'

'Sorry, what?' He was dragged from his abstraction. Aware of Jonathan's concerned glance, he smiled convincingly. 'Sorry, wasn't listening. Just looking at the pub and thinking about how long it's been here and what it must have seen,' he lied. 'What were you saying, Gordon?'

'Nae matter,' Gordon answers in his soft Scottish lilt. 'Welcome back,' he grinned.

'It was a good night, Rob,' said Jonathan as they reached home. 'Those two are splendid company, aren't they?'

'Mr Spencer!'

The man's voice said his name knowingly, and it took Jonathan aback.

'Who is it?' Both Robert and Jonathan twisted their heads toward the voice. 'What do you want?' Jonathan's panic returned.

'Sorry to startle you. It's Collins, Bob Collins, your mother's neighbour.'

It took a few moments for Jonathan to register the fact. 'Oh, Mr Collins. Of course, yes.' Then, the fear hit him. 'What's happened? What's wrong? Mum!'

'She's all right but asked me to tell you someone has burgled her home. She's a bit fraught, but okay'

'Come in, Mr Collins, and you can tell us everything.' Robert offered.

A jittery Jonathan and the two others went up to their flat.

'Please, have a seat, Mr Collins. Can I get you a drink? Anything?'

'That's very decent of you. Thank you but no thanks.' He then went on to explain that Mrs Spencer had knocked on his front door at about eight that night and said two men had forced their way into her home and threatened her.

'She asked if I could get to you and let you know, what with none of us being on the telephone. 'Of course,' I said and so drove up to the address she gave me. It wasn't too hard to find, and I remembered you from when you lived there. She didn't like asking, but that's what neighbours is for, ain't it?'

'It's after ten now. You haven't been waiting all this time, have you?' Robert asked.

'Well, yes. I … I promised to get the message to you, so I waited.'

'Oh, good heavens. Are you sure I can't get you some tea or anything?' Jonathan asked, hoping Mr Collins would decline and not waste time.

'No thanks. I'd best be off home.'

'Could I come with you? I'd like to be with mum.'

'Of course you can, Mr Spencer.'

'Here, Mr Collins,' said Robert, putting a ten-shilling note in his hand. 'Take this.'

'Oh, sir, there's no need for that.'

'It's the least we could do.' Robert said, smiling to himself at being called 'Sir' in such a pleasing manner.

'Rob, will you be all right to man the shop tomorrow? I don't know when I'll get away.'

'Of course. Don't fret. Give your mum my love.'

And they were gone. The flat was abruptly quiet, and Robert felt quite alone.

It was past eleven o'clock when Bob Collins pulled up outside his house in Whatmore Street. At this late hour, Jonathan's mother's house was in darkness. 'She must have gone to bed,' he said to no one in particular as the neighbour opened his gate and headed along the garden path.

'Oh, goodnight, Mr Collins,' said Jonathan quietly, 'and thank you.'

'That's quite alright, lad. It looks like your mum's gone to bed. Do you want me to wait awhile?'

'No. You go in. And thanks again.'

Jonathan was concerned that his knocking on the door would alarm his mother all over again, but he couldn't do anything else. He lifted the knocker and gave it three solid raps. He then called into the letterbox, 'Mum, it's me, Jonathan. Can you hear me?'

Almost immediately, he saw an upstairs light come on and a dressing-gowned and slippered woman descending the stairs. 'Is that you, Jonathan?'

'It is mum. I'm here.'

With that, he heard the hall light being switched on, the sliding back of the bolt on the door, and the Yale lock being turned. The door opened.

Jonathan stepped inside and wrapped his arms around his mother. *How frail she seems now, of a sudden,* he couldn't help thinking. 'Are you all right?'

'I'm fine, son. Fine.'

Jonathan released his hug and looked at her. 'Really? Truthfully now?'

Mrs Spencer smiled and nodded. 'It was the shock of it all. Come in and shut the door. Fancy a cup of tea?' After he had said yes, she told him to go into the front room, and she'd bring it in.

He looked about the room but could see nothing unusual. Tidy to his mother's normal, fussy standards.

'Are you staying tonight?' she called from the kitchen.

'If that's all right, mum?'

'Of course it is. You know you're welcome anytime. Your bed's always made up, in case.'

She sounded calm and matter of fact, but he was sure she would have been frightened. The tray with mugs of tea and chocolate digestive biscuits – Jonathan's favourites – soon arrived.

'So, what happened?'

'I was watching Sunday Night at the Palladium, as usual, when there was a knock at the door and two men, youngish, said they were friends of yours and were here to pick up an art book. Well, I told them you hadn't said anything to me about it, but they just pushed past me and into this room. 'Where is it?' they said. I said I didn't know what they were looking for and they started pulling things from drawers and opening cupboards. I told them to stop doing that and one of them just said to keep quiet and sit, where you're sitting now.'

Jonathan felt uncomfortable about that. 'Did they give you their names?'

'No. Then one of them went into the back room and I could hear him rummaging around in there. I went to get up, but he pushed me back into the chair. I said, 'if you tell me what it is that you're looking for, I might be able to help.' He finished rooting through things and came close to me. He put his face close to mine and growled, 'the old sketchbook. He said it was here'.

'I don't know anything about no sketchbook', I said, but I don't think he believed me.'

'You were all right, though? You weren't hurt or anything?'

'Apart from being confused and shocked, I was fine. I stayed where I was, quiet and I could hear them both upstairs going through things. Then it stopped, and they came rushing down the stairs and into the room again. One of them flicked a knife open and held it close to my face. I have to admit I was scared then.'

'Oh. Mum!'

'He said that if I was lying and hiding the book from him, he'd be back and cut me up. Then they left. It took me a few minutes to stop shaking and get myself together. Then I went round to Bob and Margie's place next door and told them what had happened. They couldn't believe it. A quiet place like Whatmore Street. I then asked Bob for a favour. Could he drive up to let you know, as there wasn't any other way being Sunday. 'Of course,' he said. And here we are. I had to tidy the place up before anyone could see it. I couldn't leave it in that state, could I?'

'Oh. Mum. Did they take anything at all?'

'Well ... some money in my dresser drawer seems to be missing.'

'How much?'

'It doesn't matter. It's gone, now.'

'Mum. How much?'

'It was to go towards the fortnight's holiday at Bognor next year.'

'Please tell me. How much?'

'Oh, don't go on, Jonathan. Ten pounds.' Mrs Spencer said it dismissively.

'Ten pounds!'

'And my post office savings book,'

'What?' shrieked Jonanthan. 'Well, tomorrow, I'm calling the police. And you must contact the Post Office to have the book cancelled. Was there much in there?'

'A little,' she lied.

At nine o'clock next morning, Jonathan and his mother were at the telephone box near the local shops where she reported the theft to the local police and to the Post Office Savings Bank Head Office. The relief shown by his mother at protecting her savings was palpable to Jonathan. They then returned to her home to await the police officers.

It was late morning when the black Wolseley pulled up outside the house and two policemen approached the house.

The officers took notes of the details and descriptions, including Jonathan's, and gave promises of a thorough investigation before leaving some thirty minutes later. That afternoon, the two of them made their way to the local post office to reaffirm the phone call made that morning and to freeze the account against unlawful withdrawal. The post office said they would issue a new savings book shortly.

'I think a nice cup of tea's in order, don't you, dear?'

Jonathan was thankful that his mother could make so light of events. He, on the other hand, remained anxious and uneasy.

When he was certain his mother had fully recovered from her ordeal and was looking forward to getting back into her normal routine, Jonathan headed off to the tube station.

'Before you go, dear, tell me. What were those horrible people looking for?'

'I honestly don't know, mum. Perhaps the police will tell you if and when they catch them?' With that, he left.

Jonathan and Robert spent a quiet night at home discussing their own events of the last couple of days and were happy to get off to bed early.

Next morning, while eating their breakfasts, the intercom from the street entrance sounded. 'Is that Mr Ferngrove, Robert Ferngrove?' the voice asked. 'This is the police. May I come in, sir?'

Robert met the uniformed policeman at the door to the flat.

'You are the keyholder for the bookshop at 26 Cecil Court, I believe, sir,' the constable stated, looking around the flat and acknowledging the presence of the other man in the room. 'I'm sorry to have to report that there has been a break in at those premises in the early hours. Your security alarm alerted us to the incident.'

'Was anything stolen?' A panicked Jonathan asked.

'And you are, sir?'

'Oh, sorry, Jonathan Spencer. Robert's partner. Business partner, that is.'

'It's impossible to say,' the constable continued, reverting his attention to Robert. 'There are books and things strewn around the shop, so we need you to come down and tell us what is missing. There's a car outside, if you'd both care to accompany me.'

When they arrived at the Court, the policeman escorted them to the shop, which had its front glass door panelled up by what looked like plywood. No other shop was open, as it was still early. Robert used his key to open the door, pushing it over broken glass and injured books. The shop was a mess. It would take them hours to go through everything.

The policeman took notes and told Robert to report the stolen items to the local station so they could decide whether to investigate it as a burglary or criminal damage. He sadly agreed.

So, once again, Robert was left with restoring order in the shop, checking to see what money had been taken from the till – he was pleased to see that no cash had been removed – and caring for their damaged stock.

Jonathan was, Robert could tell, once more in a state of shock. He was slipping further into states of anxiety and depression, finding it increasingly difficult to cope with these traumatic events and was always on the verge of emotional instability. All Robert could do was to provide Jon with as much support as possible and, of course, his unwavering love. He held Jonathan close to him and felt him crumble into his embrace. Smoothing Jonathan's hair, he then lifted his face to wipe away the tears that were now falling. He kissed his lover's soft lips tenderly.

'Ahem, excuse me again, sir.' The policeman had returned to the shop. 'I'm sorry to disturb you but forgot to mention that you should contact a glazier and a locksmith, as soon as possible, to ensure your premises are secure. I'll be off now. Mind how you go!'

Damn, thought Robert. *that's all we need.* He guided Jonathan to the stool where he had sat only a few days ago in shock. 'We need to get you home, my darling. You should sleep.'

With that thought, he picked up the telephone and called Simon Williams. 'Hello Simon, it's Robert. Sorry to call you so early but I was hoping to catch you before you set off for work. I have a great favour to ask of you …'

'My God, what's happened here?' Simon said with astonishment as he entered the shop.

'Oh Simon. I'm back here with Jonathan. Thank you so much for coming. I'm sorry for imposing on you like this, but I need someone I can trust.'

'That's quite all right, my friend. What can I do to help?'

'Would you help Jonathan back home? He's in a poor way and needs to be in bed. I have to try to sort this lot out before I can leave and report back to the police.'

'Police? What's happened?'

Robert explained about this intrusion and the other incidents which were causes for concern.

'If you can get him home and stay with him until I can get there, that would be just wonderful. Here are my keys to the flat and some cash for a cab. Is that all right? Are you sure? I'm so grateful, Simon. Thank you.'

It was some time before Robert had restored order inside the shop. Many of the books had, sadly, been damaged, some irreparably, and this caused him much sorrow, but otherwise, the shop was presentable once more. The glazier and the locksmith had done their work, so business could resume. Robert, however, felt no inclination to re-open that day, so went off to Charing Cross Police Station to let them know. After he had given his statement, he headed to the tube station and home.

When he reached home, he buzzed to be admitted into the block of flats and Simon met him at the door.

'How's Jonathan, Simon?'

'Shattered. He took a couple of pills and went straight to bed.'

'I'm so grateful to you, my friend, for looking after him. Pour yourself a drink while I go and check on him. Mine's a G and T. I'll be back in a moment.'

The two men sat for a long time, talking. Robert explained the problems he and Jonathan had encountered over the last few weeks, and Simon offered what to Robert were sincere, empathetic noises. He's such a good man, thought Robert.

At just after seven, Simon, after checking with Robert that he was feeling all right, collected his things and headed for the door.

'Give my love to Lisa. And, Simon, thank you. Thank you for looking after Jon, and thanks for being here for me. Everything.'

'You're very welcome, Robert. Glad I could be of assistance. I'll see you again soon.'

Chapter Fifteen

When Rossi and Sarah Mulholland entered the shop that morning, the words *Oh no, not again*, shot through Robert's mind. While it was last Sunday they last met up, it seemed to him that so much had occurred since then. Coincidence? Robert didn't think so.

He heard the woman suggest in the strongest terms to the small man standing by the biography section that he should leave the shop immediately. He did as he was told. She then reversed the 'Shop Open' sign on the door and joined Rossi as he approached Robert at the rear of the shop.

'Good morning, again, Mr Ferngrove.' Rossi said.

'What now?' was Robert's retort. 'I said all I have to say when we met last. There is nothing more I wish to say.'

'I think you should see this,' Rossi announced, slapping the newspaper onto the counter.

'What's this?' It was Il Gazzettino. 'It looks like an Italian newspaper.'

'Not Italian. Venetian. Have a look at the page three.'

Robert turned to the page. 'What am I supposed to be looking at?'

Rossi pointed to the following article, headlined:

'Om trovato morto a San Polo l'è annegà'

'Am I supposed to be able to read this?' Robert said, looking up disparagingly at Rossi.

'I will translate, though of course, I am Italian, not Venetian. It says:

Man found dead in San Polo had drowned

A man whose body was found in the Rio de San Zan Degola in the San Polo region died from drowning, a post-mortem test has found.

The 50-year-old's body was discovered on Saturday, with tests concluding he had suffered no injuries.

Formal identification found the body to be Guido Zampelli of San Polo.

Detectives are investigating whether the death could be linked to an assault and a robbery, which took place in Mr Zampelli's bookshop two days earlier.

'There is more, but you understand the story.'

'I certainly do. Is this your doing?'

'That is of no concern. I thought you would wish to learn of this.' Sarah Mulholland smiled mechanically at Rossi's intimation.

Robert, while saddened to know that the man he had met briefly was dead, was quite calm about the news.

'I thought also, you would care to know that your sister is doing very well in the Milan Chamber Orchestra.'

On hearing his sister mentioned, Robert's calm demeanour became less so.

'Joanna? Is she … safe?'

'Yes, she is safe. For now.'

'What do you mean by that?'

'Mr Ferngrove. I mean nothing. But one can never tell in life. People have accidents all of the time.'

'You'd better not let anything happen to her.'

'Or what, Mr Ferngrove? What will you do?' Rossi's tone became menacing, and the woman's plastic smile disappeared.

Before Robert could answer, Rossi went on. 'Do not make threats to me. You are in no position to do so. Even now, as we speak, things are happening that will bring the sketchbook to me, since you have refused to give it to me. I have offered you a very good price but still you said 'no', so now I have to follow a different path.'

'It will never be yours, Rossi. Never. It is in a safe place. Somewhere you cannot get it.'

'So you think,' interspersed Mulholland. 'My boys have been busy searching for the book Mr Rossi has told me is his. There is just one more place for them to look. They are at your flat right now.' The mechanical grin appeared again.

'Jonathan!' Robert's voice was barely a whisper.

'And, Mr Ferngrove,' Rossi's voice was also a whisper but tinged with vitriol, 'if the book is not in my possession after their visit, Miss Mulholland will report your disgusting behaviour to the police.' The smile that came to Rossi's face was not artificial. 'That will be most satisfactory.'

'What do you mean?' Robert asked, fearing the truth that was coming.

'You are a dirty homosexual, Mr Ferngrove. A queer. A pervert.'

'What makes you think that? How dare you?' Panic in Robert's voice. 'It's a lie.'

'Not according to your sister, it is not. She was very forthcoming with the information to me. So, you see, Mr Ferngrove, I do know about you and Mr Spencer.'

'Yes, who is it?' Jonathan asked into the intercom. He really didn't want visitors today. Too tired.

'Sorry to disturb you, sir. Police. Is that Mr Jonathan Spencer?'

Oh, God, thought Jonathan, what now?

'Yes, I'm Jonathan Spencer. You'd better come up,' pressing the button on the intercom to release the door to the street. He had no idea just how easy the two men pushing open the street door thought gaining access was. He was waiting by the door when the knock came.

'Detective Inspector Jones, sir, and this is Sergeant Brown,' the first man announced when Jonathan opened the door. 'We have an urgent message from Mr Ferngrove.'

'Oh, is everything all right? Come in. What is it?' Then it crossed his mind: why would two detectives come to deliver a message? Wasn't that the job of a PC?

'May I see your warrant card, please?'

Sergeant Brown closed the door with a foot. Inspector Jones reached into his pocket and produced not a warrant card but a blued steel Webley revolver, which Jonathan saw was pointing at him. His eyes widened and his mouth dropped open slightly. His heart pounded in his chest. He had no idea why he did it, but he moved his hand toward the gun. It was an involuntary action, never intended to take the gun from Jones. There wasn't time to do so anyway, as the gun and Jones's hand smacked into the side of his head.

He reeled and staggered back into the room and fell, blood dripping through the fingers of the hand he held up to the pain. He lay on the polished floorboards, just about conscious of not letting blood drip onto the expensive Persian carpet.

The two men set about their task. Brown produced a large linen bag from his pocket, and they started with the bookcase, pulling every book down and tossing them into a heap on the floor, except for any that could comply with the description given to them by their boss. These went into the bag. They opened every drawer they could find in the living room and quickly examined the contents before adding them to the growing piles on the floor.

They lifted and shifted the seat cushions and backs. Desk, table, cabinet, chairs were each in their turn treated the same. Brown grabbed a hold of Jonathan and yanked him to his feet before thrusting him into the kitchen and onto a stool. Their search continued in that room. The noise of pans, crockery and cutlery hitting the tiled floor was horrendous to Jonathan.

Then onto the toilet and the bathroom, similarly treated. The second of the bedrooms had a double divan bed, table and light, tastefully decorated Jonathan always thought. They examined all the items before throwing Jonathan into the main bedroom and onto the bed.

The two men simultaneously saw the small safe among the shoes when they wrenched open the wardrobe door. It had a combination lock. It was locked.

'Open it.' Brown demanded of Jonathan.

Jonathan was quite truthful when he said that he rarely used the safe. 'It's usually Robert that uses it. I don't know if I can remember the combination.'

Brown grabbed his lapel. 'You'd better fucking try. For your sake.'

He knew that this was where Robert kept the sketchbook. He knew also how much it meant to his partner. For his sake, he tried to be stoic. 'I can't remember. Please!'

The smack of the gun's butt on the same side of his head as the last one sent him sprawling back onto the bed. More blood.

'Open it.'

Crying, Jonathan repeated that he didn't think he could.

Brown reached across the bed and yanked him off it. 'If you don't fucking open it now, you won't have any eyes to see to do it later. Got it?'

Jonathan nodded. He knelt down at the open wardrobe door and turned the combination to the appropriate numbers and with tears and blood flooding his eyes he opened the safe door.

Brown shoved Jonathan aside and took out all that was in the safe. Money, documents, packets, everything and put them into the linen bag. He nodded to Jones who then plunged a heavy boot into the prostrate man's abdomen before hurrying out of the flat.

It took a long time and all of his effort to drag himself out of the flat and to the door of Brenda's flat across the landing. He heard her gasp 'My God!' as she opened her door but nothing more. He passed out.

～

'We are going now. I trust I will never have to see you again, Mr Ferngrove. The book will be in my possession shortly, so our business is concluded. I will not say it has been a pleasure. That is far from the truth. Goodbye.'

Rossi and Mulholland left the shop. Robert's first thought was for Jonathan and his safety. He had to get home to him. So, once again, he closed the shop early, rushed into Charing Cross Road and hailed a taxi.

As the taxi approached his Ufford Street flat, Robert saw an ambulance leaving the front of his building. The taxi pulled up behind the black Wolseley car also in front of the entrance to the flats. Paying the driver, he pushed the cab door open and ran to the entrance. A police constable stationed outside the entrance stopped him.

He told the constable his name, and the constable allowed him to proceed through the street door, which was propped open. Robert ascended the flight of stairs to the landing where, again, he came up against another police constable. When asked, Robert gave his name and said he was the owner of that flat, pointing to where his front door stood open.

'Wait there, please, Mr Ferngrove.' The policeman moved to the flat entrance, knocked and told the man appearing at the door of Robert's presence. The uniformed officer and the plainly dressed man approached the anxious Robert.

'Mr Ferngrove?' The policeman asked and when Robert confirmed this, he went on, 'I am Detective Sergeant Grant. This is your flat, sir?'

'Yes, what's happened? Where's Jonathan? Is everything all right? Is ...'

'All in good time, sir. A man has been taken to hospital. The lady from the flat there identified him as Jonathan Spencer. It was her what called the ambulance and us.' The policeman must have noted the look of horror on Robert's face, and continued, 'he's been beaten up a bit, but he'll be fine. We need you to enter the flat with me and tell us what, whoever did this, might have been looking for. All right, sir?' Robert nodded.

The scene that Robert met caused him to stumble. The policeman held his arm. He looked into his home, or rather the devastation and chaos that it now was, in disbelief.

'Please tread carefully, have a look around, and please don't touch anything. Just tell me if you think something has been stolen.'

Robert waded slowly through the debris. 'It's impossible to say until things are restored to their place,' he said.

'That's all right, sir, for now. Just anything obvious to you.'

Only upon reaching the main bedroom could Robert definitively state that someone had emptied the safe and, since he couldn't see its contents scattered about, assumed they had been stolen.

'Thank you, sir. I know this is difficult, but I need you to come with me now down to the station where you can make a statement, listing those items.'

'But Jonathan. I need to see him.'

'In good time. Now, please come with me.'

The two men with the linen bag arrived in Beaufort Gardens, Belgravia just twenty minutes after leaving the Ufford Street flat. They parked their car and walked the short distance to Sarah Mulholland's impressive looking building. All the properties in this upscale area of London were of a classical style, painted in a light cream colour, and had large white framed windows on each of the three floors. Black ornate railings and an arched doorway created an opulent impression. The buzzer admitted them to Miss Mulholland's apartment.

'Have you got it?' Mulholland asked the moment the two men entered the elegant lounge room and before Rossi could. They emptied the contents onto the polished walnut dining table.

'Careful.' Sarah demanded.

'Sorry, m'm.'

Rossi sifted through the items and opening packets. He stopped and looked hard at the two men, then at Sarah. 'It is not here.' He looked through the items again. Nothing. 'Where is it? What have you done with it? You've taken it, haven't you?'

'Whoa! We've taken nothin'. Miss, tell 'im. We've worked for you for years, we would take nothin', would we?'

'Andrea, they may be crooks, but they're my honest crooks. They haven't taken anything.'

'Unless you told them to.'

'What! Don't talk to me like that you prat. What would I want with your bloody sketchbook?'

'Yes. I know. I am sorry, Sarah. But where the fuck is it?'

Chapter Sixteen

During the short drive to Southwark Police Station, Robert's thoughts were all about Jonathan. 'Was he badly hurt? What happened to him? Will he be alright?' He sat without speaking alongside DS Grant for the full thirteen minutes it took the car to reach the police station.

The car stopped outside a three-storey, utilitarian brick-faced building. There was a central wooden blue door with a transom window above it. The ground and first floors each had five evenly spaced windows with white frames. Immediately at the sides of the entrance were large cobalt-coloured, framed notice boards with the familiar blue police lamp mounted above the door next to a crest and the words SOUTHWARK POLICE STATION.

DS Grant got out of the car and, opening the other rear passenger door ushered Robert toward that blue entrance. This took them through to a reception area, the duty officer's desk and interview rooms. Again, Grant ushered Robert towards a particular door and on to a chair in front of a plain, functional metal desk.

'Please wait here a moment, Mr Ferngrove. I'll be back shortly to take some details. Can I get you a cup of tea?' Robert declined the offer, and Grant left him in the room.

His thoughts once again turned to Jonathan. He had to admit to being worried about him, about his state of mind. He had been through a bit of late. Robert determined that when he was well again, the two of them would spend some time away from the shop to get back to normal. Perhaps a few days in Dorset would be relaxing.

Grant returned to the room, interrupting Robert's deliberations.

'I've just checked with St Thomas's, and they tell me Mr Spencer is comfortable. No serious damage, just a couple of cuts and bruises, and a bit of concussion. He'll be allowed to go home soon, the hospital says.'

'Thank you for doing that. That's very kind.'

'Now, then, sir, just as a matter of routine, I'll ask you some questions and then get you to list what you know has been taken from your home.'

DS Grant requested Robert's full name, address, date of birth, ownership status of the flat, place of work, and other general information, which Robert readily supplied. When asked if he lived at the Ufford Street flat alone, he replied that his friend, Jonathan Spencer, was staying with him for the time being.

'Why is that sir?'

'Mr Spencer is looking out for a new place and, as we co-own the Cecil Court bookshop, it seemed convenient for him to stay with me temporarily.'

'Why would Mr Spencer have been at your flat during the day this morning?'

'He hadn't been feeling well, so I suggested he stay indoors to recuperate.'

'We shall need to speak with Mr Spencer also, but perhaps, sir, if you would list here what you know to be stolen, that will be of assistance.'

A rather nervous Robert wondered aloud whether all this bother was normal for a simple break-in, to which DS Grant replied that since someone reported the matter as an attack on Mr Spencer, they had to treat it differently.

Feeling miserable, Robert wrote out the short list of items that he knew were in the safe that morning and that were now gone. Things that would be a pain to replace and/or cancel – documents, passports, cheque book, and so on – but at least he could be truthful in not declaring the sketchbook as having been taken.

'Thank you, Mr Ferngrove. We'll circulate this list of stolen goods to stations around town, but I wouldn't hold out too much hope of getting them back. If there is anything else that comes to mind … anything at all that you wish to tell us … do let us know.'

The taxi dropped Robert off in front of the large reception building of St Thomas's Hospital. The trip had taken just ten minutes, a shorter time than that taken for the reception staff to locate the whereabouts of Jonathan. He was directed to the waiting area at the Outpatient's Centre, where he sat with about twenty other people for a short while before speaking briefly with a clearly busy nurse. She said she would check on Mr Spencer, that Mr Ferngrove should sit down, and that someone would contact him soon.

Forty minutes later, a different nurse appeared in the waiting area. All eyes were turned towards her in expectation. 'Erm,' she said, looking around the waiters, 'the person for Mr Spencer?' Robert stood, and the heads of the others waiting there turned deflated back to their magazines or the floor. Would the gentleman care to go to Outpatient's Reception where Mr Spencer would shortly be deposited. It was easy for Robert not to smile at this pronouncement.

When Jonathan emerged from a corridor into the reception area, Robert felt delighted to see him, despite his battered face and bewildered demeanour. He may be physically sound to leave the hospital, thought Robert, but I'm not sure about his mental state. *The poor love's always been a little vague, but now he looks positively disorientated.* He hurried over and placed a loving hand on Jonathan's arm. 'Hello, you.'

Jonathan gave a wan smile before looking away from Robert's face to the exit. 'Can we go home?' He murmured.

'Of course,' Robert replied as consolingly as he could but felt alarmed at the apathy being shown by his partner.

In the taxi, Jonathan said nothing, just stared ahead of him, and when they stood at the front of their building, Robert saw a look on Jonathan's face that he interpreted as fear. 'It's alright, heart. There's nothing to be afraid of. The flat's a bit of a mess but I'll get that tidied up.' Robert thought *again* and continued, 'come on, I'll make us a nice cup of tea first.'

'Sorry, Robert. Thank you. I'm just being a bit silly. A cup of tea will be nice.'

At the door to their flat, Robert heard Jonathan's staggered breathing and placed an arm around his waist, pulling him close to comfort him as he opened the door. Jonathan gave a quick intake of breath as he looked into his home and saw the mess again. He stepped forward bravely, Robert thought, being careful not to tread on anything.

'Oh, Robert. I'm sorry but I couldn't stop them.'

'No, don't blame yourself, heart. It most certainly wasn't your fault. I'm just sorry that you had to go through this.'

'They took things from the bookshelf and the cabinet drawers, and ...' here Jonathan hesitated, 'I guess you know, from the safe. The safe, Robert. Everything in it. Everything. The sketchbook included.' His voice broke.

'Don't fret. It's alright. They didn't get the sketchbook.'

'What!' Jonathan's voice was incredulous.

'Yes,' Robert continued, 'I removed it. It's in safekeeping elsewhere.'

'Not here?' Jonathan seemed to find the news difficult to comprehend.

'That's right,' Robert pronounced.

'Is that what they were looking for? Just the sketchbook?'

'Yes, I think so. We foiled them again.' Said a jubilant Robert.

'So, I went through this horror show for nothing? Why didn't you tell me? Why did you let me suffer like this? That bloody sketchbook. I wish we'd never found it.'

'Hey! Steady on. I didn't know Rossi would come here, and I just didn't get a chance to tell you that I'd moved it. Come on, sit at the table. I'll put the kettle on.' Jonathan acquiesced.

The tea seemed to relax Jonathan a little, and Robert felt his lover's anxiety subsiding. Robert told Jonathan again that the sketchbook was no longer in the flat but didn't elaborate and Jonathan didn't ask about it. They discussed the practicalities of notifying the bank of the chequebook loss and the need to retrieve copies of documents and so on. 'And, of course, the police will need to talk with you about Rossi being here. Descriptions and all that.'

'But he wasn't. It wasn't Rossi. It was two thugs pretending to be policemen. That's why I let them in. They said you had agreed to them coming here.'

'Then, they must have been that Mulholland woman's men. Either way, the police will want to know. You'll be all right with that won't you?'

'I expect so. Come on, let's get this place tidied up a bit.'

'Scotland Yard. How may I direct your call?'

'Chief Superintendent Mount, please'

'May I say who's calling.'

'Sarah Mulholland.'

'Hold the line caller. I'll see if he's free.'

'Mount.' The voice was detached, his mind clearly on other things, Sarah felt.

'Hello, Sweetie. Sarah here,' her voice tinged with a mixture of mirth and malice.

His voice lowered in volume and in timbre. His attention would now be hers alone. 'Miss Mulholland. What can I do for you?'

'I need you to do something for me. Can we meet?'

'Certainly. Where? When? I'm a bit tied down with a murder investigation right now, but I'll get away.'

'The café on Victoria Street. You remember the one?'

'Jeez, Sarah, that's miles away. I don't know I can spare that long away from here.'

'Oh, I think you will, Sweetie. One hour from now. I'll see you there.' She hung up.

'Andy, my dear, I don't think you should come with me to meet this man. We have a special kind of relationship that you don't need to involve yourself with. You're welcome to stay here if you wish?'

'No, grazie. I will return to my hotel and wait for your call telling me of that little shit's arrest.'

She told her two henchmen to take the 'crap' off her table and get rid of it. They did so and left. Then Rossi departed. Sarah freshened up, put on her light overcoat and left the apartment, too. The weather she found to be a little cool and crisp but no rain, so she decided to walk the mile to her destination, along Lower Grosvenor Place, past the Royal Mews and left into Victoria Street. Arriving early, knowing Mount wouldn't arrive for at least fifteen minutes, she entered the café, where the staff greeted her obsequiously as a recognised and well-respected patron.

Twenty minutes later, Mount came through the front entrance. She watched as he glanced around the room before coming over to her table. She didn't stand but pointed to the seat opposite her. Mount sat.

'Want a coffee?' she asked.

'No thanks. I have to get back. What do you want, Sarah?' He reached into his jacket pocket and extracted a packet of Senior Service, offering Sarah one, which she declined. He lit his from a gold lighter.

'I want to tell you about two filthy queers that need to be dealt with. Properly, legally, so that the press is interested enough to run a story about them.' And, with that, she proceeded to tell Mount all she knew, and more, about Robert Ferngrove and Jonathan Spencer.

Mount stubbed out another cigarette and folded his notebook away. 'Right. I'll put a report in and get word out to their local nick. Are they something to you, Sarah?'

'Not likely. They've annoyed a business associate of mine and need to realise they can't do that sort of thing. Not when they're fucking shirt-lifters.'

'Okay,' Mount said, smirking. 'Can't stand that sort either. We'll have 'em. Anything else?'

'Not for the mo', thanks. Just phone me when you've made the arrests. Here's a little something for the next copper's charity ball.' She handed the policeman a small, slightly bulky buff envelope, which he slipped into the inside pocket of his suit jacket before leaving and slipping into the waiting vehicle outside.

The murder investigation took up the rest of the day, so Mount decided to file the report on Ferngrove and Spencer the next morning.

He was at his desk early, typing out the report, which he would take up to the Records Department a little later.

'Good morning, sir,' the civilian records clerk seated at the front desk rose sharply and greeted Mount. 'How can we be of assistance?'

'I'm here to lodge this report.' Mount announced, showing the clerk his document. 'And here is my identification.'

'Thank you, Chief Superintendent.' The clerk checked that the report had been completed per procedure and gave Mount an acknowledgement of submission. The senior man hated what he considered this bureaucratic pedantry but knew it was necessary and was grateful he had others in his department that would normally do this sort of thing, but this was different.

'I'll enter the details into our books as soon as I can today, sir. Thank you.'

The clerk noted the names on the report for cross-checking with existing records, which he would arrange when practicable. Later in the day, he registered the crime and placed Chief Superintendent Mount's report in a new file. The clerk wrote brief details about the file – file reference number, reporting officer, date, the code for the crime type, and crime location, his own name – on the label adhered to the folder, then completed a Notice of Crime slip which he placed inside a buff-coloured internal memorandum envelope. Having noted to which district station the slip was to be delivered, he wrote 'Southwark' in neat handwriting on the front and placed the envelope into the courier basket for collection and disbursement on Monday morning.

Neither Jonathan nor Robert slept well on Friday night and were tired and not a little tetchy the next morning.

'Well, at least we've got the place looking respectable again, although the breakages and damage are horrible. Don't let your toast go cold, Jon.'

'I won't. Don't nag please Robert.'

'Sorry, I'm sure.'

After a few minutes of uncompanionable silence, Robert announced, 'It's eight thirty. I'd better get cracking if I'm to open the shop at a reasonable time. Are you up to coming in?'

'Not really, Rob. I don't think I'd present well to customers, and, besides, didn't you say that the police wanted me to make a statement thingy? Will that be today, do you think?'

'Yes, that's right. I don't know when, though. It might not even be today. Do you want me to wait here with you, just in case?'

'That would be nice. But I know you've got to get the shop open. Don't worry about me, I'll be alright here on my own. You go.'

Robert sighed and thought, *don't do this please Jon. Playing the martyr doesn't suit.*

'If you're sure, then I will.' And he went off to get ready, while Jonathan sulked over his cold toast.

The police didn't come to the flat and Jonathan felt he had wasted his day but simultaneously was grateful for the peace and quiet their non-attendance bestowed upon him. Robert returned home at just after six o'clock. It had been extremely quiet in the Court, so the two of them were able to swap disappointments about an unproductive and tedious day.

Sunday, too, came and went with no sign of the police. The two men spent a mundane day at home, agitated. Jonathan was still a bag of nerves over what he had suffered of late, while Robert felt a gnawing restlessness, a sense of being on edge, being divorced from his sketchbook. Neither of them had a pleasant day; the bangs, flashes and whizzes of the evening's Guy Fawkes celebrations did nothing to help either.

Robert went to work the next morning, glad to have something to divert his fixation from the sketchbook. He wondered again whether he had done the right thing removing the book from his presence, but knew had he not done so, it would have been lost to him forever.

It was ten o'clock when the intercom to the flat buzzed. 'Mr Spencer? Police. May we come up?'

Jonathan panicked. 'How do I know you're the police? That's what the last lot said. How can I be sure?'

'I have a uniformed officer with me. Are you able to look out of your front window down to the street? I'll get him to stand across the road so you can see him.'

'All right.'

'Jeez, what a palaver. Jones, get out of the car and stand over the road.' After a few moments, Detective Sergeant Grant returned to the intercom and buzzed. 'Did you see my officer, Mr Spencer?' When Jonathan said he had, he released the latch, and the policeman ascended the stairs to the flat.

'Warrant card please,' demanded Jonathan, holding the door marginally ajar. He allowed the detective into the room when satisfied, even though he still felt anxious. 'Sorry, officer.'

'That's quite all right, Mr Spencer. I can understand your wariness. Are you able to come and give us a statement at the station now? I'm assuming you're feeling okay?'

'Yes, I am, thanks. I'll just get my things. Will you be able to bring me back afterwards?'

'I think we can arrange something.'

Jonathan walked through the same entrance to Southwark police station Robert had the previous Friday, for the same purpose. He, too, was shown into Interview Room 2 by DS Grant and, as his partner before him, declined the offer of coffee or tea.

'Right,' began the police officer, 'let's get some details about what happened.' Jonathan was asked a number of questions regarding the attack – 'Yes, sir, we're treating this as aggravated burglary, a bit more serious than just burglary' – and his responses were written down by Grant on a report form. Like most police officers, Grant was efficient yet empathetic, so that Jonathan felt a little more comfortable as he relayed the events of the attack.

It was about twenty minutes into the interview that the knock came to the room's door and the balding desk sergeant appeared at the entrance. 'Excuse me, sir.'

'Yes, sergeant, what is it?'

'A word, if I may.'

Grant apologised to Jonathan, rose and went with the sergeant out of the room.

'What is it, Brian?'

'We received this NOC this morning. Thought it might be relevant to your enquiries.' Sergeant Brian Glover handed the crime notice to DS Grant.

Grant looked at the names on the notice, and the crime code listed. He glanced at Glover, then back at the notice. 'Is this what I think it is, Brian?'

'Gross indecency, Peter. You've got yourself a poofter in there.'

'Now then, sergeant, that's no way to speak about these sorts of people. You know the Met's line on handling 'out of the ordinary' persons, and the collective responsibility we are required to adopt.'

'Of course, sir,' the sergeant said, smirking, I beg your pardon. I should have said 'We've got ourselves a poofter in there.'

Chapter Seventeen

'Hello, Records Office? DS Grant from Southwark nick here. I'd like a file sent down as soon as you can, please.' The detective gave the clerk the file details from the Notice of Crime slip, then waited.

'Ferngrove and Spencer. Yes, that's the one. Can you have it sent right away, please? Thanks. Oh. Who lodged the report? Who? Phew! Thanks again.'

Grant hung up and left the main office for the Interview Room, collecting a uniformed constable as he went. Jonathan turned in his seat and saw the policemen enter. Grant moved towards the table while the other man stood close by the door.

'The two men were impersonating police officers. I forgot to mention,' Jonathan announced with some pride in remembering. 'Brown, and Jones, I think. Yes.'

'Jonathan Spencer. I'm arresting you on the charge of gross indecency. You do not have to say anything, but it may harm your defence if you do not mention when questioned something which you later rely on in court. Anything you do say may be given in evidence.'

'What? What, I don't understand? What do you mean?' Incredulity then panic showed in Jonathan's voice.

'Constable, take him down to the cells. We'll be speaking again in a little while, Mr Spencer.'

'No. No, this isn't right. Wait. What about my attack? I don't understand. What do you mean?'

Frightened and crying, Jonathan was led out of the room, through a further door off the reception area and down some steps to where six open cell doors were awaiting. He was led by the arm into the first cell, which measured about 8 feet by 6 feet. There was a wooden bench to one of the white-tiled walls. It stood on cold, hard concrete. The bench held a blanket and an uncased pillow. A small, barred window sat high up on an outer wall. The smell of disinfectant and mustiness from a lack of proper ventilation made for an unpleasant smell that assaulted Jonathan's collapsing senses.

He sat on the bench and the heavy metal cell door thumped shut as the police officer left him there. Shock and bewilderment manifested themselves in his thumping heart and tightened throat. Swallowing became difficult and he had a strong urge to defecate. Jonathan clutched the edge of the bench as he sought some stability within the chaos. His eyes darted around the bland and impersonal room, and he tried in vain to find sense in a senseless situation. He lay down on the bench and sobbed.

DS Grant knocked on his superior's door.

'Come.' DI Compton's voice sounded rougher than Grant knew its owner to be. He had got to know George Compton well in the twelve months they had been together in Southwark and had a great deal of respect for the man, though, if he was honest, some of his policing methods were old hat. Not surprising, given his age.

'Sir, we've got an incident downstairs that you need to be aware of.'

'Oh? What is it, Peter?'

Grant handed the man the NOC. 'The report's on its way to us, sir, and we have Spencer in custody.'

Compton removed the pipe from his mouth and gave a look that suggested to Grant that something unpleasant had crawled along his moustache and died there. 'You don't need me for this do you?'

'Normally, I wouldn't bother you, except the report was lodged by Chief Superintendent Mount at the Yard.'

Compton's look changed to one of bemusement. 'Was it, indeed?' He placed his fountain pen onto his blotter. 'What's in the case of a couple of queers to interest the Chief Super, I wonder? Better play this strictly by the book, Peter. Keep me informed, won't you? Just in case.'

Grant went to the main office to await the couriered report and busied himself with other paperwork in the meantime.

It had gone six when Robert Ferngrove opened the front door to his flat. It was dark inside. 'Strange. Jon. You here?' No answer. He switched on the overhead light and made for the kitchen, thinking there would be a note for him. Nothing. He hastened to the bedroom, fearing the worst, but, again, nothing. 'Where the hell is he?' The knock at the front door startled him. He walked towards it. *Left his key at home again*, he thought. He opened the door, ready to throw a hug at him. It wasn't Jonathan.

'Thank God you're home, Robert.' It was Brenda from the flat opposite, and in response to his querulous look she said, 'the police have taken him away.'

'Oh, that's alright, Brenda. They said he needed to make a statement about the attack.' Robert thought, *that's where he'll be.*

'But that was this morning. I haven't heard him come back. Not that I'd pry.'

'Of course not. Don't worry. I'll drop into the police station to see what's happening. Thank you for caring, Brenda.'

'That's all right, Robert. If you need anything ...' And she was gone, back to her flat.

Robert left a few minutes later and walked the fifteen-minute journey to Southwark Police Station. It was cold, but Robert was glad there was still no rain. He was a little concerned that Jonathan was taking so long at the station, or that perhaps he had gone on somewhere after giving his statement, *but surely, he would have phoned me at the shop.* He was still running options through his head when he reached the station and entered through the now familiar front blue doors into the reception area.

'Good evening, sir. How can we help you?' The uniformed officer asked.

'My … friend … came here today to give a statement, and I wondered whether he was still here.'

'What name, sir?'

'His name is Spencer. Jonathan Spencer.'

There was a pause before the officer asked, 'and you are?'

'Robert Ferngrove.'

'Please take a seat over by that wall, Mr Ferngrove. I'll make some enquiries.'

Robert sat and the police officer departed his desk. He returned a few moments later. DS Grant accompanied him. 'Mr Ferngrove. DS Grant. You may remember me?' Robert did. 'Come through to this office.' Robert moved to the same office in which he gave his statement. He didn't sit.

'DS Grant, I think Jonathan Spencer was here to give a statement today?'

'That's correct, Mr Ferngrove.'

'Is he still here? May I see him?'

'He is no longer here. We moved him to Brixton nick.'

'Moved? What do you mean, moved?'

'He was arrested for gross indecency. He has made a statement in which he names you, sir, and then he went to Brixton, as I said. And now, Robert Ferngrove I am arresting you also on the charge of buggery under the Offences Against the Person Act of 1861. You do not have to say anything ...' Grant again recited the obligatory caution.

Grant caught Robert as his legs gave way in shock. He sat him down on one of the interview room chairs.

For some time, Robert couldn't utter a sound, and his furred gaze towards the far wall of the room saw nothing. No thoughts came to mind. He could make no sense of what he had just been told. DS Grant let him sit there until he had to repeat that he, Robert, had been arrested and was required to go with him into a cell downstairs, but he didn't, couldn't move.

'I shall take a statement from you shortly, Mr Ferngrove, but in the meantime, if you would please come with me.'

A constable helped Robert up and escorted him down to, coincidentally, the same cell in which Jonathan had been detained. He, too, stared vacantly at the same tiles that his love had done several hours ago.

Robert sat on the same cold, unforgiving bench that Jonathan had been on. The weight of the situation pressed down on him, as heavy as the metal door that confined him. His mind raced as he struggled to make sense of the events that had led him here. A gnawing anxiety clawed at his insides.

Each thought was a jagged edge, slicing through his composure. *Why now? Why us?* The unfairness of it all stung sharper than the chill of the cell. He couldn't help but think of Jonathan – *how had he coped with this same suffocating dread?* The thought of Jonathan being moved to Brixton, alone and frightened, wrenched at Robert's guts even more. His hands trembled slightly as he clutched the edge of the bench, again mirroring the actions of his loved one.

What if I can't convince them we aren't criminals? What if this ruins everything? The fear of the unknown gnawed at him. Each unanswered question generated a fresh wave of panic. His heart pounded erratically, and his anxiety heightened with every minute.

Robert forced himself to breathe deeply, focusing on the thought that had kept him grounded through all these years: his commitment to Jonathan. He clung to the hope that their truth, their love, would somehow prevail in a world that seemed determined to tear them apart.

The cell was a physical manifestation of his fears – cold, confining, relentless. Yet, within him, there flickered a stubborn ember of defiance, a refusal to let this moment break him completely. He resolved to face what came next with the same quiet dignity he and Jonathan had always lived by.

That was his anchor in the storm. That was his flicker of hope amid the overwhelming darkness.

It seemed hours later that a constable opened the cell door. 'All right, pervert, time to go back upstairs.' Robert looked forlornly at the officer, slowly rose and moved toward the door. 'Don't you fucking touch me, you faggot. You sort of people are disgusting. Revolting. Get up those stairs.' Robert looked with sadness at the man.

Another constable met him and led him into the Interview Room, where DS Grant was waiting. 'Sit down, Mr Ferngrove. I want you to make a statement regarding the offence you have been charged with, but first I want you to be sure you understand why you have been arrested. Do you understand the term 'buggery' or 'gross indecency'?'

'Yes, I understand. I also understand that the law's wrong when otherwise innocent people are treated as criminals.

'It's not even as though we have a choice in the matter you know. No one would elect to be homosexual. One either is or isn't. It's how we are born. Like the colour of your eyes.'

'Save your speeches for the statement, Mr Ferngrove. You may be right or not. It's not for me to say, nor does it alter where we are right now, which is that you need to make a statement relating to the charge. Are you ready to do so?'

Following Robert's reluctant agreement, he made the following comments, which DS Grant took down in his meticulous and neat, left-handed slanting handwriting:

I, Robert Ferngrove, residing at Flat 5, 33 Ufford Street, Southwark, hereby provide the following statement voluntarily and of my own accord.

I have been living with Jonathan Spencer, at that address, for the past two years approximately. We co-own a bookshop business called Ferngrove and Spencer, located at 26 Cecil Court, London, WC2. Our partnership has always been one of mutual respect and shared interests, focused primarily on our business and our quiet life together.

Jonathan and I have always conducted ourselves with discretion and respect for those around us. We have never sought to draw attention to our personal lives, and our relationship has been adult, private and consensual. Our primary concern has always been the wellbeing and success of our bookshop, which has I believe become an accepted and welcome part of the Cecil Court community.

It has been made clear to me today that a third party, whose name has not been made known, has reported our relationship to the authorities. This has caused great distress to me, as Jonathan and I have always strived to lead our lives with integrity and without causing harm to anyone.

I wish to make it clear that while our relationship is genuine and has always been conducted in private, I acknowledge it is illegal under current law. I reiterate, however, that our actions have not caused harm to any other person or violated their rights.

I am prepared to cooperate fully with any police investigation and to provide whatever information I can to assist the police. My sole desire is to continue to live quietly with my partner and to contribute to our community and society through our business.

[Signature] Robert Ferngrove [Date] 6th November 1961

'What happens now?' asked Robert

'You, too, will be transferred to Brixton for detention, pending trial or bail. It's unlikely that you'll see Mr Spencer. It's a large facility.'

'What about things at home? And the shop?'

'I'm sorry but you'll have to take that up with your solicitor or whoever.'

The handcuffed transfer from Southwark Police Station to Brixton in the Black Maria had not gone well for Jonathan, who appeared to be in considerable distress to anyone who cared to notice. Not that anyone did.

He stood, shaking and silent as the logging in process was gone through, then he was pushed along to one of the cell lines and into the fourth cell along. His handcuffs were then removed, and he was dumped onto the wooden bench that represented both seat and bed. He collapsed sideways along the bench as tears flooded from him and wouldn't abate, and now he shivered uncontrollably. He stared with blurred eyes at the white tile wall opposite. Words and sounds, none of which made sense, tumbled about in his mind. Logical thought eluded him. Panic. Fear. Horror. Each simultaneously dominated his emotions. He called out in despair, 'Robert!' Then more quietly, 'Mum.'

Chapter Eighteen

'Hello, Sarah. Mount here. You asked me to let you know when Ferngrove and Spencer had been arrested and charged. They have. And there's more. One of them, Spencer, has topped himself.' He ended the call.

Sarah placed her telephone on its cradle and consulted her little book of telephone numbers. She put the book back into her handbag and dialled a number.

'Hello. Dickie Watson, please. Yes, I'll wait. Hello, Dickie, Sarah. Got your pen handy? I've got a story for you about two queers that you need to get into the paper as soon as. No, sorry, no politicians or nobility involved this time, just your basic sleaze crap, though one of them has died. You ready? Okay, these are the details...'

Having been transferred to Brixton Police Station, Robert realised that this must have been the exact procedure that Jonathan had undergone. The connectivity gave him some comfort, even though the thought of Jonathan having to go through all this on his own distressed him.

Upon his arrival at the rear of the building, Robert was led out of the transport and into a secure area of the custody suite. In the booking-in area, Robert was processed with fingerprints and photographs taken. He was informed of his right to legal representation to which he requested a call to his own solicitor. Robert saw that the time was now after nine-thirty, and as he only knew the name and location of the legal firm's office, he would have to look up the number. He was told to wait until the following morning before finding the number and making the call.

He was then led to one of four cell lines and 'invited' to enter cell eight. Unlike the quiet cells at Southwark, the noise of voices and shouts hit Robert's senses from other cells in the line, the thumps of doors being closed together with the pungency of disinfectant, sweat and piss. It was unpleasant.

Despite the hour, the police orderly brought him a tray of sandwiches and a mug of tea. Robert couldn't eat anything though, and it was removed early next morning when his breakfast of toast, butter, jam, juice and coffee replaced it.

Unsurprisingly, Robert hadn't slept well. He had feared what may happen to him and he was deeply worried about Jonathan. He hoped to see Jonathan but doubted they would let him.

He again asked about phoning his solicitor, and after a few minutes was led out to a designated consulting room where via Directory Enquiries he obtained the phone number of the legal representatives and got through to Colin Thompson, who, once appraised of Robert's situation, dropped what he was doing and set off to see him immediately.

It was over two hours before Robert was led from his cell to the small, stark consulting room. His solicitor was already seated at the table, a briefcase open in front of him. He looked up as Robert entered, then stood to greet his client albeit with an expression that was a mix of concern and determination.

Colin Thompson was a family lawyer of about forty years of age. Tall, and made seemingly taller by his thin physique and long neck. He had a full head of dark, wavy brown hair brushed directly back from his face, and eyes that displayed empathy and warmth. He wore a dark blue suit, white shirt and striped tie, all befitting his profession.

He had overseen numerous legal transactions for Robert, and for Jonathan, including the negotiations for the shop and flat leases.

'Robert, please sit down.'

Robert dropped onto the chair opposite Mr Thompson, the weight of the situation pressing down on him. 'Thank you for coming, Mr Thompson. I'm scared and don't know what to do.'

Mr Thompson nodded, his eyes kind but focused. 'Let's start with the details. You told me briefly over the phone what has happened but now I need you to go over everything thoroughly.'

With a trembling voice, Robert took a deep breath and recounted all that had occurred since he had come into the police station to report everything about the attack. 'I came in looking for Jonathan, who had made a statement about the attack earlier in the day but hadn't come home yet. I couldn't believe it when they charged me. Me! All of a sudden, I was the villain, not the victim. It wasn't right. I told them so, but it didn't make any difference. They didn't want to know.'

'Did they mention any specific evidence? Witnesses, perhaps?'

Robert shook his head. 'No, just that they had evidence. They didn't show me anything. It's my belief that the attack was not the main reason for those thugs turning up at the flat. A man named Andrea Rossi was after an item of mine and was prepared to do anything to get it. Including blackmailing us over our – Jonathan and my – relationship. He's the one the police should be after. Him and his cohort, Sarah Mulholland.'

'Sarah Mulholland's in on this, is she?'

Did Robert detect apprehension in his solicitor's voice?

He continued with his explanation of events while Thompson made copious notes until, finally, he sighed and closed his notebook. 'Alright, Robert. We'll deal more with that in due course. For now, we need to focus on your first appearance in court, scheduled for tomorrow morning. I'll prepare the necessary documentation and argue for bail, though given the charge, it might be difficult.'

Robert's eyes conveyed his worry. 'What about Jonathan? He must be terrified.'

Mr Thompson reached across the table, reassuringly touching Robert's arm. 'I'll contact Jonathan as soon as I leave you. He's apparently here in this nick, so I'll explain the situation and make sure he's alright. You need to focus on staying strong for him.'

Robert nodded, though the fear and guilt gnawed at him. 'Thank you, Mr Thompson. I appreciate your help. I suppose you should let my parents know, too. Oh, and Joanna. She's in Italy. I don't have her address or a phone number with me. Perhaps my parents have the information. I'm really not sure.'

The solicitor gave him a small, encouraging smile. 'Don't worry, Robert, I'll deal with that. Stay positive. We'll get through this, Robert. One step at a time. Now, let's go over what will happen tomorrow.'

They spent the next hour discussing the procedures for the first court appearance. Thompson explained the importance of the plea, the chances of bail, and what to expect in the courtroom. Robert listened carefully, trying to absorb every detail.

As their meeting drew to a close, Mr Thompson packed up his briefcase and stood. 'I'll see you in court tomorrow morning. Stay strong, Robert. We'll fight this together.'

Robert watched as Mr Thompson left the room, a glimmer of hope flickering in his heart. It just wasn't fair. They'd done nothing to hurt anyone, just lived ordinary lives, quietly, peacefully. He was still terrified but knowing that he had someone fighting for him made the burden a little easier to bear.

The guard escorted him back to his cell, the door clanging shut behind him. Robert lay down on the hard bench, staring up at the ceiling. He thought of Jonathan, hoping that Mr Thompson's visit would bring him some comfort. As he closed his eyes, he whispered a silent promise to himself: he would endure this for Jonathan's sake, but he knew he could only plead one way.

The next morning, he was brought before the magistrate's court for his first appearance. He wondered when Jonathan's appearance in court would be.

The magistrate, a stern and ancient-looking man with a no-nonsense demeanour, read the charges aloud. 'Mr Ferngrove, you are charged with buggery under the Offences Against the Person Act of 1861. How do you plead?'

Robert's voice was steady, though his hands trembled slightly, and he felt his legs wouldn't support him for too long. He looked down at his feet as he responded. 'Guilty, Your Honour.'

The magistrate had received prior notice that Robert would enter a guilty plea and announced to the court that he would refer sentencing to a higher court. He then turned to the matter of bail. The prosecutor argued against it, citing the seriousness of the offence and the public interest. Colin Thompson argued for bail, highlighting Robert's excellent character and lack of prior offences. After a brief deliberation, the magistrate denied bail, and Robert was remanded in custody.

Robert sat on the narrow bed in his cell, the cold, damp air pressing in around him. He stared at the small window high up on the wall, a sliver of light barely penetrating the gloom leeched onto the tiles of the cell walls. Already, days had begun to blur together, each one a monotonous repetition of the last. He had become oblivious to his surroundings, the sights and sounds of prison activity going on around his cell. He clung to the hope that one day, things would change, that he would be free to return to Jonathan.

The sound of footsteps echoed down the corridor, growing louder as they approached his cell. Robert looked up as the guard stopped, then slid open the Judas window to check on his prisoner. The guard then opened the door. He had a grim expression on his face.

'Ferngrove,' the guard said, his voice low. 'You've got a visitor.'

Robert's heart leapt. *Jonathan!* He stood up, his legs unsteady and followed the guard down the maze of corridors to the visiting room. As he entered, he saw Mr Thompson, his solicitor, waiting for him. Robert was disappointed. The look on Mr Thompson's face was concerning.

'Mr Thompson,' Robert said, his voice trembling. 'What's happened?'

Thompson took a deep breath; his eyes filled with compassion. 'Robert, I'm afraid I have some terrible news. Jonathan... Jonathan appears to have taken his own life.'

The words hit Robert like a physical blow. 'What!' He staggered back, his hand clutching the edge of the table for support. 'No... no, it can't be. That's not right. Jonathan wouldn't...'

Mr Thompson reached out, placing a comforting hand on Robert's shoulder. 'I'm so sorry, Robert. You told me that Jonathan was in an extremely emotional state. He clearly found coping with all this: the stigma, the threats from Rossi, and now your arrest too hard to bear.'

'How ...? No, I don't want to know. When? Where? Suicide?'

'I don't have too many details, except this newspaper item appeared today.' He showed the paper to Robert.

PRISONER FOUND DEAD IN CELL

Prisoner Jonathan Spencer, 34, of Ufford Street, Southwark was found dead yesterday, hanging by strips of clothing attached to the window bars of his cell at Brixton Prison.

Spencer was due to appear at Marylebone, London, as was his partner, Robert Ferngrove, also of the Ufford Street address, to face a charge of gross indecency.

Both men ran a prosperous fine bookshop in London's Charing Cross area.

Tears welled up in Robert's eyes, and he sank into the chair, his body shaking with sobs. 'I should have been there for him. I should have protected him.'

Mr Thompson sat down beside him, his voice gentle. 'There was nothing you could have done, Robert. Jonathan was overwhelmed by the situation. Being involved in this matter was too much for him.'

Robert buried his face in his hands, the weight of his grief and guilt crushing him. 'How can you possibly know! You're only my bloody solicitor. You don't know anything about Jonathan. He was my everything. How can I go on without him?'

The solicitor sighed, his own eyes glistening with unshed tears. 'You must find the strength, Robert, for Jonathan's sake. He wouldn't want you to give up. We will continue to fight for you, to appeal your sentence. But you must hold on.'

Robert nodded, though the pain in his heart felt unbearable. 'I'll try, Mr Thompson. For Jonathan. Sorry.'

As the guard led him back to his cell, Robert felt an emptiness inside him. The world had lost its colour, its meaning. He slumped onto his hard bed and cried for a long time but then knew he had to be strong to honour Jonathan's memory. He would endure the darkness, the isolation, the stigma, the looming imprisonment and, one day, walk through those prison gates.

But then it hit him. The thought. The doubt. The dread. 'Was it suicide, or was he got at? Did Rossi, or rather, Mulholland, have enough clout with the police to do this?' He didn't know, and frankly, at this moment, it was irrelevant.

'Got a minute, Sir?'

'What is it, Peter? Come in.'

Compton put his pipe down in the ashtray and beckoned his sergeant to sit down.

'Thank you, sir. Do you recall the other day we had the two queers in here, the ones that the Chief Super had an interest in? Well, one of 'em's topped himself in Brixton nick.'

'Poor blighters'

'The queers, sir? I didn't think you'd be sympathetic toward them.'

'Not them, Grant. The chaps at the nick. Poor sods'll have a hard time of it. Good job it didn't happen here.'

'You're dead right there, sir. But ... I know the official line is one of zero tolerance to this sort of thing, but there are lots of coppers who are privately unsure about criminalising homosexuality. There aren't many, and they would never go against the book, of course, but some do have their own perspectives shaped by personal beliefs, experiences, and the social circles they move in. The more artistic ones among 'em especially.

'Some officers even see the laws as being harsh and the suffering they cause. I know some quietly turn a blind eye and advise individuals on how to avoid detection or even express support for the decriminalisation of homosexuality.'

'There hadn't better be any sympathisers in my nick.' Compton replies. 'The legal framework of this country positions homosexuality, quite rightly, as a criminal offense, and the Met are tasked with enforcing those laws.' He harrumphed. 'Homosexuality is not only a moral failing but also a threat to public order and decency. The police are under pressure to uphold societal norms, which are heavily influenced by conservative and religious values. This leads to a proactive approach in identifying and prosecuting homosexual acts. And if raids on known gay meeting places, such as public restrooms – 'cottages' – and private clubs, are necessary, then so be it.

'It's a sickness, Peter. A disease. And we must work with other institutions, including the judiciary, to ensure that those convicted of homosexual acts receive harsh penalties, and that includes imprisonment. The police will also cooperate with the media to reinforce the notion that it is a societal menace. Sorry about the rant, but there it is'

'Gosh, sir, I didn't realise you were so against queers.'

'Well, I am. I have little sympathy for these people and that is a view shared by a good number of my contemporaries, with many of us feeling justified in our actions, which represent prevailing moral standards. Where will the world end up if we give free rein to these degenerates? We're already seeing societal standards slip because of this rock and roll music and beatniks lazing around coffee shops and giving a lot of cheek and abuse to not only our men but the public at large if they deign to show disagreement with their deviant ways. I tell you, Grant, I didn't fight a war to allow our Christian beliefs to be lambasted.'

'You know I would never dispute your word as my superior, but I do have more modern ideas about how society is developing since the end of the war. Attitudes are certainly changing and there are greater opportunities for younger people today. Look at how many cadets the Force is now taking on.'

'I'm sure we could debate this till kingdom come, Peter. I'm just glad I'm nearing retirement and won't need to face your 'brave new world'.'

'Sorry, sir, I didn't mean to turn this into a debate. What I wanted to say was that as Spencer, the one what hanged himself, as well as Ferngrove, were processed here initially, we may be drawn into the inquiry that is bound to take place. There's a possibility you may be involved.'

'Damn! Yes, of course, thank you, Peter. That's all I need. Close the door behind you.'

'Thank you, sir. Oh, and, of course, we won't be doing anything else about the attack on Spencer, now.'

Chapter Nineteen

'Andy, Sweetie. Have you heard? The two queers have been arrested and one of them has done himself in.'

Sarah heard the quick intake of breath over the telephone line. 'Is it Ferngrove?' he asked.

'No, the other one. He was a mess, mostly because of you.'

'Me? I was never interested in him. It was Ferngrove that I had a problem with.'

'Well, the police think the blackmail and threats were a major factor in it. I think we should talk, don't you?'

Sarah knew the police wouldn't be interested in pursuing the blackmail and attacks on the two homosexuals for two very good reasons: They were homosexuals, and she was the influential Sarah Mulholland. But Andrea Rossi didn't know that they wouldn't be following up on things. *Unless,* she thought, *my friend Mount wanted to do so.* She grinned. 'You come to my place. You know where I am.'

She hung up the receiver and wondered how long it would take him to get here. How concerned was he about the supposed difficulties she had put him in?

He arrived two hours later. *Keen, then,* she thought. There wasn't a great deal of warmth between them. This was purely business.

'Come in, Andy. Nice to see you again.' There was little sincerity in Sarah's voice.

'I have been thinking in the taxi on the way here that you may still be able to do something for me.'

'And what might that be?'

'I still want the sketchbook. It is hidden somewhere, I don't know where, but you could have your people continue to look for it, no?

'I don't think so, Andy, sweetie. I'm not going not spend any more time looking for your precious book.'

'But, why not. It is still important for me to have that book, and ...'

'It's taken up far too much of my time and I have incurred a lot of costs, so I think it is now time you settled your account with me.'

Rossi was incredulous. 'What do you mean? Pay you? I did not think that was the arrangement.'

'Whether you did or you didn't, darling, that is the arrangement now.'

'How much?'

'Three grand will do it.'

'What? That is over seven million lira. You are out of your mind.'

'That's the cost of keeping you out of jail, sweetie. The police know you are the one that was blackmailing those two queers, so it's going to cost to stop them arresting you.'

'How do they know I had anything to do with those two? Hey? How?' Rossi sneers. 'They do not know.'

'Oh, but they do. I told them.'

'What! Why would you do this? I thought we were friends.'

'And so we are, but this is business. We can still be friends after you've paid up.'

'Madre di Dio, sei una bisbetica, una fottuta strega.'

'Yeah, whatever you say. I expect to see proof of your payment into my bank account within twenty-four hours.'

'Twenty-four! That is impossible, even if I agreed to do so.'

'Oh, you will. Should you choose not to, there will be repercussions. The Metropolitan Police will be visiting you, but not until my boys have left their calling card. I would recommend that you do as I say and get the money to me without delay. She handed Rossi a piece of paper with some bank details on it. This is a special account. Make sure you pay it there.'

'This is blackmail.'

'Is it?' Sarah asked in mock surprise. 'You should know, sweetie. You're the expert, supposedly.'

Rossi glared at her. 'I do not like being conned like this. I thought I could trust you.'

'Trust? Why should you trust me? We have done business before, but that is just what it was. Business. Trust doesn't come into it. Twenty-four hours, Andy. You'd better be off, the clock's ticking. Goodbye.'

After he had slammed the door behind him, Sarah was on the phone. 'Benny? Yes, it's me. I've got a little watching job for you ...'

Rossi was still seething with anger when he got out of the cab, threw the fare at the driver – 'Oi!' – and shoved his way past an elderly couple standing at the hotel entrance. He demanded his room key from Reception and, once in possession of it, stormed over to the lifts, pressing the button repeatedly. People looked in amazement at this uncouth behaviour.

Back in his room, Rossi stalked the floor, going nowhere, just burning off the fire in his mind. Gradually, both the pacing and the anger dissipated as ideas came to mind. One especially kept returning to him. *Leave. Leave, now.*

But what about the sketchbook? – That would have to wait – What about the payment to Mulholland? – No chance – What about being arrested? – Not if I leave now – Mulholland's men? – Same.

It was the plan. Rossi was riled not to have the sketchbook, but he considered his freedom to be more valuable than seven million lira. Seven million! She's out of her mind.

He picked up the phone, calmer now. 'Hello Reception, would you please get me the telephone number of Alitalia. Yes, the airline. Thank you.'

When he received the information, he rang them without delay. 'When is the next flight to Milan and are there seats available? ... No, that is too soon ... Yes, that is the one. Will you please book me a seat, Business Class if you have it ... You do, thank you.' He gave the girl the details she asked for. 'Yes, one-way. I will pay you when I reach the airline counter at the terminal. Would you please repeat the flight details and booking reference. I will write them down. Thank you. Yes, I will be at the counter before the two hours before embarkation. Where is the Business Class lounge located? Excellent. I shall see you then.'

'Hello, Reception. Please have my account ready for settlement. I shall be leaving in one hour's time.'

Packing complete, Rossi rang for a porter and went to Reception to settle his bill. He withdrew his traveller's cheques from his jacket pocket and began filling in the details. The nod the receptionist gave to the man close to the entrance was imperceptible. 'Thank you, Mr Rossi. I trust you have had an enjoyable stay with us. We look forward to seeing you again very soon.'

Rossi indicated to the porter to take his bags to the taxis waiting outside the front door and headed that way himself. It was several hours before his flight, but he felt it best to be ensconced in the lounge as soon as possible.

'Mr Rossi?'

The voice was East End local. He knew later that he shouldn't have responded to the enquiry but impulsively he turned to face the person.

'Not thinking of leaving us, are you, Squire? I don't think my employer would be too happy about that.'

'You can tell your employer that she can go to hell.'

'That's not a very nice thing to say about a lady, is it?'

'Out of my way.'

He was stopped from advancing further by the frame of the stocky Londoner. The physical contact told Rossi that the man was fit and strong. His face suggested he was not averse to even greater physical contact.

He hissed at Rossi. 'Miss Mulholland said to remind you that the Metropolitan Police, bless their hearts, would want to have a word with you. I guess what with you leaving, that chat might well take place at the airport, unless of course you wanted to come with me right now and collect the dosh what she's expecting from you?'

'Tell her that I have to make arrangements with my bank in Italy to have that sort of money transferred.'

'I'll tell her, but she said to let you know she has contacts all over this very small world who are thrilled to do as she asks. Get my drift? Twenty-four hours.' He stood aside and Rossi wasted no time getting into the taxi and heading for the airport.

❧

'Meeting. Now. Drop what you're doing and come over here.'

Two young policemen and one policewoman left their desks and followed their superior into the designated area.

'What's up, Sarge?'

'We've had a tip off that some Italian 'gentleman' is about to head off home without having first satisfied the Chief Super that he's alright to do so. He's legging it today. We've got to stop him.'

'Do we know how he's travelling?'

'Not for sure, but apparently, he's in a hurry, so I expect it'll be by air. So, the first thing to find out is which airlines are flying to Italy today.'

'Do we know which city, Sarge?'

'Nope. So, a bit of policing's required. You remember what that is, Smith?'

'Yes, Sarge.'

'Report back with your findings in half an hour, or sooner, if you're lucky enough to find anything.'

In precisely twenty-three minutes, the three officers were knocking on their sergeant's door.

'What've you got for me?'

'Right, Sarge,' Peters declared, 'we've identified five airlines that fly to Italy today. All are from Heathrow. Of the five, two have already taken off and don't have further flights until tomorrow. Of the three that are left, BOAC has two flights – one to Rome and one to Milan. BEA has four flights – two to Rome, one to Milan and one to Florence. Alitalia has five flights still to go – Rome, Milan, Venice, Florence and Naples.'

'So, he's got to be on one of those flights.' A smug Smith announced.

'Right, Peters and Amanda, come with me. Smith, you stay here in case we need an anchor.'

Thirty-five minutes later, they had pulled into the car park of the Air Ministry Constabulary at Heathrow. It irked Sergeant Watson immensely that he had to defer to what he considered were partially trained police officers, not much better than civil servants. It was they who held the jurisdiction over the airport.

Showing his warrant card, the uniformed sergeant asked politely to see the officer in charge.

'Right, sir. Constable Lewis is on call. I'll show you through.'

Watson explained to Lewis that he was looking for a man that was likely to abscond to Italy this afternoon and they needed to find him and interview him.

'Splendid,' Lewis replies. 'Do you know where to find him?'

'No. We are planning to seek the assistance of the various ticket counter operatives. We have three airlines that we want to speak to. Will that be alright?'

'Absolutely. Do you need me with you? Except I've got a bit on this afternoon.'

'If you give us the okay, we'll be happy to proceed.'

'Righto. You've got it.'

And with that, the three Metropolitan police officers headed for the Europa Terminal.

'Right,' the Sergeant said, 'Amanda, you take Alitalia. Peters, you take BEA. We need to know if Rossi's booked on a flight. I'll take BOAC. Meet back at that counter when you're done. Any questions? Off you go.'

The passenger traffic at the Alitalia check-in counter was steady. WPC Philpott approached the counter from the side and spoke to an airline staff member.

'Hello, may I speak with the Manager or Supervisor. Thank you … Good afternoon. You are?'

'Helena Joyce. I am the supervisor. How can I help you?'

'We're looking for a passenger that we believe may be booked on one of your flights to Italy this afternoon. Unfortunately, we don't know which one and were hoping that you could show us the reservations for each of the flights.'

'Of course. Come through.'

'Reservations are made in physical ledgers, or reservation books, with each page representing a specific flight, date and time. The names of each passenger, a unique Passenger Name Record, seat assignments and other pertinent details were logged. What name are you looking for?'

'Rossi. Andrea Rossi.'

Helena looked at the first manifest. 'We have three flights scheduled for take-off this afternoon or early evening and a further two this evening. The first is AZ400 to Rome, via Paris.' She ran her finger down the list of eighty booked passengers. 'Rossi, Rossi … Yes, here, Mrs Mariana Rossi. Is this the person?'

'No,' the policewoman replies. 'It is a man we are seeking'

'Oh, yes, sorry. That is all for this flight.' She turned the page to the next flight details. 'Flight AZ465 to Milano. Departure time 17.05.' She again ran her finger down the passenger list. 'Rossi, Andrea. Yes, he's here.'

'That's great. Has he booked in yet?'

'Yes. He is in Business Class, so you may find him in the Business Class lounge, or Club Aspire Lounge, as it is called, that our airline has access to.'

'That's worth a try. How do I get there?'

'It is located through security. You need to follow the 'All Airline Lounges' sign, and keep left where more signs show, 'Lounges B-J'. The Club Aspire Lounge is signposted Lounge D on the right. But you will need me to accompany you.'

'Okay, Helena, but first we must meet up with my sergeant at the BOAC counter. Is that okay? Good.'

The two women set off briskly. Sergeant Watson was waiting with Peters and was pleased to receive Amanda's result. The two officers were introduced to Helena Joyce, and her role was explained. That done, they set off for the Club Aspire Lounge. Accessing the security area caused no delay, and they entered the lounge.

The three police officers looked about the lounge area while Helena explained to the Lounge reception staff what was going on. It was then they realised they didn't know what Rossi looked like. They asked the reception staff if they could identify the man but having said they couldn't, but they could send a message for him to come to reception.

When Rossi responded, several minutes later, somewhat hesitantly, to the call, he was taken aback to see the uniformed police officers. Sergeant Watson moved towards him. 'Mr Rossi? I have been instructed to speak with you prior to you leaving this country.' Turning to the reception staff, he asked, 'Is there a quiet room we can use?'

He gestured to Rossi to move toward the room indicated, leaving Peters and Philpott in the Lounge area.

'Am I under arrest?'

'No, sir. I am not instructed to arrest you but to give you a message from Chief Superintendent Mount of Scotland Yard. He wants you to know that he knows about your indebtedness to Sarah Mulholland and about your involvement in the attempted blackmail of two persons. He has also said that both the police and Miss Mulholland, personally, have contacts in Italy that will act upon their instructions should you fail to conclude your arrangement with her. I am sure you are aware of that which I speak?'

'I am, officer. And let me tell you, neither Miss Mulholland, nor your police force scare me. I shall, however, be dealing with the matter first thing tomorrow. You may be an obedient little messenger and run back to tell your boss that. Now, if there's nothing further, I will bid you arrivederci and continue my journey home.'

Chapter Twenty

you for letting me know, Mr Thompson. Is there anything I can do? Should I come home?'

'There isn't really anything you can do for Robert right now, Miss Ferngrove. I have advised his ... your mother and I believe she will be visiting him at Brixton Police Station as soon as practicable. He misses you, I know, but, frankly, there isn't any need for you to come back to London.'

'I shall be there for his court appearance, though, Mr Thompson. Do you know when that will be?'

'Not until the New Year, I'm afraid. I will let you have the date when I know it.'

'The New Year! That's two months away. What is happening to the shop? To their ... his home?'

'I have those things under control. Robert granted me leave to visit the flat to collect certain personal items, and the shop to ensure that it is locked up and the goods secure. The landlords to both properties have been appraised of the situation, and both have granted me temporary provision to look after their investments. I rather think, though, that they will not allow Robert to continue his tenancy at either property given his now criminal status.'

'Criminal status! How ridiculous is that? Robert's no more a criminal than you or I.'

'That, unfortunately, is the law, I'm afraid, Miss Ferngrove.'

'How did the police get to know about their relationship, anyway? It's not as if they advertised the fact that they were living together.'

'They received a tip-off.'

'Oh no! From whom? Do we know?'

'Yes, a Miss Sarah Mulholland.'

'Never heard of her. How was she connected to Robert and Jonathan?'

'I believe she got to know them from another person. A man she was working with.'

'Do we know him?'

'Umm, hold on a sec, I'm just checking my notes. Yes, his name is Andrea Rossi.'

Silence.

'Hello, are you still there, Miss Ferngrove?'

Several seconds later, Joanna confirmed she was but needed to go.

'I will telephone you again a little closer to the Court date, but you now have my office's telephone number. If there is anything you wish to speak to me about in the meantime, do let me know.'

But she had already hung up.

~

'Good morning, Mr Rossi. I am telephoning to make sure you know to have the money sent to Miss Mulholland today.'

'Who is this? How did you get my number?'

'That is unimportant. What is important is that you honour your obligation, and I and my colleagues are here to make sure you do. One of them is already standing outside your home, just waiting to escort you to your bank, or wherever you keep your money. It is now 8.30, so your bank will be open. Please leave now and go.'

'And if I don't?'

'You don't want to ask stupid questions like that, Mr Rossi. I think you know how accidents can happen in this country.'

Rossi put down the receiver. He recognised he had no choice if he valued his life, which he did.

A few minutes later, he left his apartment and headed down the street towards his bank, hoping the fresh air would help keep his mind alert. He looked around him but saw no one that appeared to be watching him, but he couldn't be certain. Rossi entered his bank in Loreto fifteen minutes later and returned to the street ten minutes after that. He considered hailing one of the many cabs waiting in Via Nicola Antonio Porpora but decided he would prefer to walk back. Before he could do so, two men approached him from behind and guided him to a car sat along the same street, into the rear of which he was 'invited' to sit.

'I guess you belong to the same person who called me earlier?'

'Did you make the transfer?'

Rossi realised he had no choice but to cooperate. It was too late now for heroics on his part. 'Yes, I did.' It hurt him to say.

'Show me proof.'

Rossi produced a bank transfer confirmation for six million, eight hundred and seventy-four lira.

'Jesu, I did not know it was that much. Okay, you can go now. Our job is done. Arrivederci.'

Rossi left the men and hailed his taxi. He wasn't in the mood for walking now. He had some serious thinking to do.

It took quite some time for the feeling of disbelief to leave Joanna after she had put the phone down. She realised then that she must have appeared very rude to

Mr Thompson, and for that she was sorry. But. Andrea mixed up in her brother's utter ruin, not to mention poor Jonathan's death, the realisation was too much to absorb. She sat at the dining table, bewildered. This man who had done so much for her, had all along, been conducting a siege on Robert's life simultaneously. The duplicity was disgusting. How dared he?

He has been manipulating me all this time, simply to get close to Robert. The bastard. But then, but he's been so good to me. The orchestra introduction, the first-class travel, the flat. He cared. He must have done. He did! Didn't he?

She continued to sit at the table, staring at nothing, her mind churning with sorrow and new distaste for this man *I trusted him!* She now felt betrayed and belittled. *Was I only a pawn in his game to get hold of that blasted sketchbook?* Her chest tightened. *I loved him. I would have given him anything. Everything. Oh, Andrea, why did you have to be like this? I feel such a fool. Bastard. How dare you make me feel like this? How dare you be so provocative? How dare you make me love you?*

She wouldn't cry. She couldn't anyway, she was too angry.

What do I do now? Do I give all this up, my life here in Milan? If I stay, it'll feel as though I'm living a lie, a fabrication of Andrea's doing. This is all down to him. I can't continue in a fantasy of his making. I can't. Her sigh was deep and mournful. *No. I can't. I will resign from the orchestra and this flat, and return home to England, as* soon as practicable. Robbie may need me. I should see mum, too. She must be sick with worry.

So, Joanna, with huge regrets, made up her mind on the course she was to take.

Joanna. Yes, Joanna. I must make contact with her again. Where is the orchestra? Is it still undertaking promotional activities? I can't recall. Roberto will tell me.

Rossi spent a good twenty minutes on the telephone speaking with the orchestra's director and learned that the out-of-town promotions had ended and that they were taking a few days' rest before coming back for rehearsals. Roberto told him how well the local towns had greeted the orchestra and its members and had enjoyed the impromptu small orchestra interludes that he, Rossi, had proposed. He was, he said, looking forward to getting together with him to discuss the forthcoming winter programme.

So, she is back. Good. I'll drop by and see her. Yes, she can be of great help to me still. He thought about phoning her first, but decided against that, as he wasn't sure how much she knew of what had happened with her brother and his 'friend' and whether she had any negative ideas about his pursuit of the sketchbook.

Rossi was still angry at having to part with so much money, with nothing to show for it. He must find a way to get the book, and soon, as he also needed to get back to work and devote some time to recouping his losses. It then occurred to him it had been over seven weeks since he had been in his office. He couldn't let such neglect continue without serious financial ramifications.

'Hello, Joanna,' he beamed as the door was opened, and Miss Ferngrove presented herself before him. 'How are you?'

He could see her struggling to say something in response and he wasn't sure whether her face was projecting a feeling of welcome or distaste.

'May I come in?'

'You want to come in? You think it is acceptable to visit me and be pleasant? Do you? I know what you've done, Andrea, and I don't know what I can say to you without punching you.'

'I think I understand your feelings, Joanna, but please let me come in and tell you my side of events.'

He was surprised and relieved when she opened the door further and stood back, allowing him access to the room. 'It's your flat. Or, at least you had a big hand in getting it for me. I can't honestly stop you.'

'Oh, no, Joanna, the flat is yours for as long as you need it.'

'Well, I can tell you now that it won't be for very much longer.'

'Why? Are you leaving for some other flat?'

'Andrea! You bloody well know that I know about your disgraceful treatment of my brother. And what you have caused Jonathan to do is despicable. Reprehensible. There is no way I wish to be associated with you any longer.'

'But Joanna, please let me explain. It isn't how you think. I did not tell the police about your brother's behaviour. I admit I threatened to expose him if he did not see good sense about the sketchbook, but it was simply that. A threat. I did not carry the threat out. It was Sarah Mulholland who told the police. She has some hold over a senior man at Scotland Yard, and she obviously believed that she could earn merit with him by telling him about your brother.'

'That's rubbish, Andrea, and you know it.'

'No, Joanna, please believe me when I say that it was she. Hah, she has even blackmailed me into paying her a fortune. Seven million lira. She is the bad person here, not me.'

Rossi's pathetic appeals for Joanna's sympathy didn't have much of an effect on her.

'You have been in this insane pursuit of a sketchbook that Robert owns. You had me believing you in your ownership claim. Going against my own flesh and blood to support you. Well, no more.'

Rossi could see she was close to tears and moved towards her to comfort her. 'Joanna, please don't cry. Let me ...'

'Get away from me, you horrid man. I don't want you near me. You have made me look foolish, too. Have led me on, thinking that you were doing something special for me, when all the time you were using me to get at Robert. Or, more specifically, that blasted sketchbook. What's so special about it, anyway? No. Don't tell me; I'm truly not interested.'

'But Joanna, don't lock me out of your life. We can still be friends. Lovers. Can't we?'

'Lovers! Are you mad? I don't even want to be associated with you. Any thoughts of deeper feelings I may have had are long gone. I won't hate you, though. I can't, not after what you have provided for me here in Milan, but it's all in ruins now. You have broken my dreams, as well as those of Robert, and most certainly those of Jonathan. I think you should leave.'

'Please don't be hasty, Joanna. Take a little time to think about what you might do. You are well regarded by Roberto for your musicianship. You have a bright future ahead of you with the orchestra. Don't throw that away.'

'Go.'

He was steered to the door. 'Oh, and Andrea?'

'Yes?' he replied hopefully, turning to face her.

'Goodbye.' And the door was closed in front of him.

Rossi was now angry at the manner in which he had just been brushed off. *How dare she do this to me? Me, who has done so much to help her and now she is leaving the orchestra. How will that make me appear in Roberto's eyes? She's only been here a few weeks. Hell, she hasn't even performed in concert. Well, at least rehearsals haven't begun yet.* He made his disconsolate way home yet remained determined to pursue matters with Robert Ferngrove as soon as he could.

Joanna checked her diary. She had two weeks until her rent on the flat became due. Rossi had paid for the first two months, and now she felt a pang of guilt about leaving. The pang was, however, just that. Then she was over it. So, two weeks to finalise things here. She would contact the letting agent in the morning to advise them of her imminent departure for England. She would then contact Roberto and resign her post.

After that, she would write to her mother and explain that she was coming home and would be staying with her parents for a short while, if that was agreeable. And could she please send some money to her bank account to enable her to book seats on the trains home? There was no way she would consider flying with her precious cello cargo.

In a way, she felt happy to be going home. She had loved her short time in Italy, but she realised that, like so many British, leaving her homeland had been a wrench. She refused to allow Andrea's influence to plague her thoughts. *What's done is done. Time to move on.*

Next morning, Joanna did all that she had planned and set about organising her rail journey by visiting the travel agency in via Padova and working out a schedule.

Her mother's letter arrived five days later. In it she expressed joy at the thought of her daughter coming home but tinged with sadness that it hadn't worked out as Joanna had hoped. Money had been sent as requested.

On Friday, 24th November, Joanna, her cello and what little belongings she had left for home.

Chapter Twenty-One

Over the next few weeks, Mr Thompson worked tirelessly to prepare for the sentencing hearing. He met with Robert regularly to attempt to discuss the case and review the pre-sentencing reports that detailed Robert's background, character, and the circumstances of the offence. But, as ever, Robert presented a vacant and disinterested demeanour.

A suggestion of Thompson's, which he offered as an option to prison, was the possibility of female hormone therapy, otherwise known as chemical castration. This treatment was part of the broader, misguided belief that homosexuality could be 'cured' through medical intervention, whereby the administration of hormone treatments would reduce libido and sexual activity. If Robert preferred this option, it could be presented to the court as part of their plea for leniency.

Robert just shook his head. 'I have read about how Alan Turing had undergone chemical castration as an alternative to prison and what it had done to this war hero in terms of severe physical and psychological damage, which led to his death in 1952.'

He also said that knew a boy in his late teens who underwent aversion therapy with electric shocks. 'The boy told me he had been convicted of gross indecency and ordered to undergo treatment to avoid prison. He had described how electrodes were attached to his leg and shocks applied as he was forced to watch photographs of men and women in various stages of undress, the aim being to encourage avoidance of the shock by moving to photographs of the opposite sex. It was apparently hoped that arousal to same-sex photographs would reduce, while relief arising from shock avoidance would increase interest in opposite-sex images.

'He said the shocks' intensity would vary and were painful and stressful. He had to submit to these sessions for six weeks, each lasting thirty minutes. Since completing the treatment, he had become extremely depressed and anxious, but no one had followed up on his condition. He was left to face a life devoid of sexual feelings, which have never returned.'

'There is no way, Mr Thompson, that I will subject myself to that indignity.'

The sentencing date was set for two months later at the Central Criminal Court – the Old Bailey.

Without objection, Thompson instructed a barrister, Martin Collins, to represent Robert at the higher court. Much of what was happening around him, as well as to him, was a blur to Robert. His thoughts were constantly on Jonathan, what he had caused that poor, poor man to do, and how he had ruined their lives with his obsessive need to cling to that sketchbook. Some had called his desire for the sketchbook a passion, but he now knew that the drive was more than that. He knew it was an unhealthy compulsion but one which he had been unable to control. Unable or unwilling? He couldn't say.

Why did I let myself get so entwined in the mystique of that book? To become a victim to the spell it had cast. I'm so, so sorry.

Spectators packed courtroom number twelve to capacity, filling every seat to witness the trial of a disgusting pervert. The air was thick and stifling, a mix of body heat and the lack of proper ventilation, making it feel almost suffocating. The room was hot and airless, the oppressive atmosphere adding to the tension that hung in the air.

Old wood smells and musty paper blended with the faint scent of sweat from the gathered crowd. The wooden benches, worn smooth by years of use, gave off a faint, earthy aroma. The smell of ink and parchment from the legal documents added to the olfactory mix, creating a familiar and uncomfortable environment.

Noises filled the room, a constant background hum that never entirely faded. The low murmur of whispered conversations among the spectators and the press who waited like vultures to hear about the dirty goings on of a seemingly respectable man, the rustling of papers as lawyers prepared their notes, and the occasional creak of the wooden benches as people shifted in their seats. Footsteps echoed through the room as court officials moved about, their shoes clacking against the hard floor. Now and then, a cough or a sneeze would punctuate the air, drawing brief glances from those nearby.

The atmosphere was charged with curiosity, judgment, and a hint of fear. Spectators – a mix of curious onlookers and those with a vested interest in the case – watched intently, their eyes fixed on the proceedings. The tension was palpable, a silent undercurrent that everyone could feel but no one dared to acknowledge openly.

Robert Ferngrove stood in the dock, the sombre grey suit, white shirt, and floral tie contrasting with his pallid countenance feeling the weight of every gaze upon him. The oppressive environment mirrored the gravity of his situation, adding to the sense of isolation and vulnerability he felt as he awaited his fate.

Though his father's absence cast a pall, he felt a surge of happiness seeing his mother there with Joanna, too. He was glad she was able to be back from Italy for a while. He wondered whether poor Mrs Spencer knew about the trial. Had anyone thought to tell her? His attention was drawn back to the proceedings.

'All rise.' Came the command from the clerk of court. All did.

The judge made a grand entrance into his courtroom. A tall, gaunt, yet imposing figure in his black robes and powdered wig, he commanded the attention of all present. He acknowledged both prosecuting and defence counsels and sat. The court sat.

Looking sternly at Robert, he announced, 'Mr Ferngrove, you have pleaded guilty to the charge of buggery under the Offences Against the Person Act of 1861. This court must now determine an appropriate sentence.'

A murmur went around the room. The judge nodded, making a note on the papers before him. 'Yes, Mr Mortimer.' He addressed the prosecutor.

A sharp-eyed man with a clipped tone stood and addressed the court. 'Your Honour, the defendant's actions are a clear violation of the law. Such behaviour is not only illegal but also morally reprehensible. The police have been vigilant in their efforts to curb such activities, and this case is another testament to their diligence. This court owes it to them to support their efforts and eradicate this subversive and despicable behaviour. A sentence that reflects the seriousness of this criminal activity is required.'

As he sat, the prosecutor's words hung in the air, a stark reminder of societal attitudes. Robert's barrister, Martin Collins, a compassionate man with a calm demeanour, rose to speak at the invitation of the judge.

'Your Honour, my client has shown genuine remorse for his actions. He is a man of good character, and this is his first offence of any kind. My client has lived a quiet, discreet life, causing no harm to others and has suffered much loss and trauma in the last few weeks. I urge the court to consider leniency in its sentencing.'

The judge leaned back in his chair, contemplating. He removed his spectacles and looked directly at Robert. 'Mr Ferngrove, the law is clear on matters of buggery. However, I will take into account your early guilty plea and the circumstances presented by your counsel. Nevertheless, the determined stance of the police and the public interest in this case cannot be ignored.'

The courtroom was silent as the judge's words sank in. Robert's heart pounded in his chest, each beat echoing in his ears. He glanced around the room, seeing the faces of the spectators, some filled with curiosity, others with disdain. His mother looked down while Joanna was watching him. She gave a half smile. He felt a wave of despair wash over him, knowing that his life would never be the same.

'Mr Ferngrove, the court must consider the severity of the offence and the need for deterrence. The law is clear, and the punishment must reflect the seriousness of the crime. In its pre-sentencing report, the Prosecution sought to have behavioural aversion therapy applied. Having considered this matter at length, I do not think this appropriate. I therefore sentence you to eighteen months' imprisonment. Two of which have already been served in custody. Take him down.'

'Court is adjourned,' the clerk announced as the judge took himself out of the court.

Robert felt a wave of utter despair wash over him as he was led away, knowing that his life would be forever changed. The courtroom buzzed with whispers and murmurs as the spectators filed out.

Robert's barrister and solicitor approached him in his holding cell beneath the court, the latter placing a reassuring hand on his shoulder.

'We'll appeal, Robert. We'll do everything we can.'

Robert nodded, though he knew the chances were slim. The law was the law, and society's views on homosexuality were harsh and unforgiving. His thoughts continually returned to Jonathan and what he had inflicted on the man he loved. And his parents; how would they cope with the news? How would they survive the ignominy of this ordeal?

The two men departed, and the jailer slammed the cell door shut behind them. After waiting motionless for what seemed like mere minutes in the holding cell, and feeling numb and disorientated, the prison van arrived at the rear of the courthouse. The cold, metal doors a stark reminder of the reality that awaited him. Robert, handcuffed, climbed inside, the door clanging shut behind him. He sat down on the hard bench, staring out of the small, barred window as other prisoners were loaded into the transport before setting off. The city of London passed by in a blur, the familiar streets and buildings now seeming distant and foreign.

As the van made its way through the city, Robert's mind wandered back to the events that had led to this moment. He thought of his partner, the love they had shared, the quiet moments of happiness they had stolen in a world that refused to accept them. How could something so pure and beautiful be deemed a crime? The injustice of it all burned in his chest, a mix of anger and sorrow that threatened to overwhelm him.

The van pulled up at the prison gates, the heavy iron doors creaking open to admit them. Robert was led out, the guards' hands firm on his arms as they guided him through the maze of corridors and cells to be processed. The sound of metal clanging against metal echoed through the halls, a constant reminder of the confinement that awaited him. Wormwood Scrubs.

His cell was small and bare, with a narrow bed against one wall and a small window high up that let in a sliver of light. Robert sat down on the bed, the reality of his situation sinking in. Sixteen more months. It seemed an eternity. How would he endure it? How would he survive the isolation, the stigma, the constant fear of prisoner attacks, that he was sure would happen.

As the days turned into weeks, though, Robert found a routine of sorts. His days began early, with the harsh clang of the morning bell echoing through the cold, damp corridors. He stood by his bed, waiting for the guards to complete the roll call, his breath visible in the chilly air.

Breakfast was a grim affair, the porridge tasteless and the bread stale. He ate quickly, avoiding the hostile stares of other inmates. The dining hall was filled with the murmur of low conversations and the clatter of metal trays, a constant reminder of the oppressive environment. It was here that Robert encountered what he considered the worst possible type of homosexual.

He had met other sympathetic men in the Scrubs but Maisie – real name Martin – was the sort of queer that Robert abhorred. Openly homosexual and seemingly not caring if anyone knew he was queer, he flaunted around in a group of similar boys, girly and quite outrageously effeminate and made a beeline for Robert being the new queer on the block. He was quick to let Maisie know that although both were homosexual, he was not the same as him and while Maisie feigned drama at such a rejection, Robert knew that mental distance was vital to his sanity. The fact that Maisie and his cohorts ostracised him from their group at mealtimes did not concern Robert in the slightest.

Work assignments varied, but Robert often found himself in the laundry, the heat and steam a stark contrast to the cold of his cell. The work was hard and monotonous, but it provided a brief escape from the isolation. He kept his head down, focusing on the tasks at hand, trying to avoid drawing attention to himself.

Lunch and dinner were similarly unremarkable, the food barely enough to sustain him. The afternoons were spent in the workshop, where he learned basic carpentry skills. Education programmes were a small glimmer of hope, a chance to learn something new and plan for a future beyond the prison walls.

The smell of dampness and disinfectant was ever-present, mingling with the stench of men's bodily functions. The noise of the prison was a constant background thrum; a reminder of the many lives confined within its walls.

Healthcare was basic, and while Robert had access to regular check-ups, the mental strain of his situation was something he had to endure alone. The stigma and isolation weighed heavily on him, but he found strength in the hope that one day, things would change, both for him individually and others like him, collectively.

The nights were the hardest, the silence and stench of the prison pressing down on him, the darkness a constant reminder of his isolation. He would lie awake, staring at the ceiling, his mind filled with thoughts of Jonathan, the life they had shared, and the future that had been stolen from them.

But even in the darkest moments, there was a glimmer of hope. The knowledge that he was not alone, that there were others like him, fighting the same battle, enduring the same hardships, while people like Simon Williams championed their cause in the media. It was a small comfort, but it was enough to keep him going, to give him the strength to face each new day. As was the prospect of his weekly visit from Joanna or mother, or, occasionally, a friend like Simon.

Chapter Twenty-Two

One thirty-minute visit per week wasn't very long to commune with family and friends. It wasn't possible, for example, for Mrs Ferngrove and Joanna to visit simultaneously, so it was vital that each visit was pleasurable and to look forward to. Robert's father did not visit. Nor did he write or pass on his best wishes via either his wife or daughter.

Robert learned about what he regarded as unbelievable sacrifices made by Joanna on his behalf from his mother on one of her prior visits, but it was Joanna herself that came each other Saturday.

'Hello, Robbie. How are you? Coping alright?' She gave him a permitted hug and kiss on the cheek. Only the guards noticed.

'Hello Jo. Thanks for coming again. It's so lovely to see you. Yes, I'm doing okay.'

'You're still looking a bit thin. You eating well enough?'

'As well as one can expect.'

'I've brought a few more things, including the cigarettes that you ask for. You haven't started smoking, have you?' She handed over a paperback book, some toiletries, sweets and the cigarettes.

'No,' he gave a little laugh, 'they're currency in here. I can buy things with them.'

'Oh, I see. Well, I'll get you some more next week.'

'Um, no, not next week, Jo. I've got another visitor lined up for then, so I'm going to have to skip you next time. Sorry.'

'Gosh, don't be sorry, Robbie. Anyone I know?'

'I don't think so. Simon Williams. He's a newspaper man. He's written some wonderful articles. He's been a good friend to Jon ... to me ... for quite a while now. Someone we ... damn, I ... can trust.'

'If there's anything you'd like me to do, you've only to ask. You know that don't you?'

'Thanks, Jo. You've done so much already. Clearing out the flat and managing the stock from the shop. It's a great relief that you've been able to work with Mr Thompson over these things.'

There was a sadness, not unexpectedly, in his voice, as Robert once again pondered the losses that he had endured. Then, more stoically: 'Anyway, tell me what you've been up to since last week.'

'Nothing really. I'm writing to a few orchestras, again, to see if they may be interested in taking me on but nothing so far. I didn't say that I'd been with the Milan orchestra. I really want to draw a line under that whole time.'

'Oh, Jo, I'm so sorry. I brought that on you with my pig-headedness. In hindsight, I guess I should have let your Rossi have the book and ...'

'Not my Rossi, Robbie. Not after what he and that other woman has done to you and Jonathan. I didn't realise just what a manipulative bastard he was.'

'Nonetheless, all the nastiness could have been avoided if only I had had the strength to overcome the hold the book had over me, but I couldn't. It possessed me, Jo. It took Jon's death to make me realise I had to do something about it. And I have.'

'So, you're going to get rid of it? But isn't it worth a lot of money?'

'It probably is, but if I could bring myself to sell it, there is always a chance that Rossi would get his hands on it after all and now, more than ever, I am determined he won't.'

'What are you planning?'

'I can't say right now, but you'll know soon enough. I am set on this course of action. It'll be my form of contrition for Jonathan's death. I will never get over that, Jo. It'll be something that I will have to live with for ever, but at least there can be some atonement.'

They both sat in a comfortable silence for a few moments, before the bell indicating the end of the visitor period sounded, and each went back to their separate worlds.

By the time the next visitor session came around, Robert was clear in his mind what he wanted to do regarding the sketchbook. Any doubt had dissipated and now he was keen to put his idea into practice.

Robert watched as Simon Williams entered the room with all the other visitors, located Robert, and went to greet him.

'My dear friend. How's this awful place treating you?'

'Hello, Simon, so lovely to see you. Not so bad, I suppose, under the circumstances. Thanks so much for coming. The family alright?'

'Pretty good. Angela has been rather ill these last few weeks, and it looks like she may need an operation, poor lamb.'

'Nothing serious, I hope?'

'Poliomyelitis. Thankfully, only a mild version, but the cost of medicines! You have no idea!' Simon shook his head but smiles. 'She's worth it.'

'Absolutely, she is. And I hope I didn't drag you away from her. I really do appreciate you coming here. I wasn't sure whether you'd be put off by me asking you to come to The Scrubs.'

'Not at all, Robert. It's good to see you again. I only wish it was in better surroundings.' He looked around him, gesturing at the walls, the bars, the guards.

'Simon, I have something I want you to do if you'd be so kind. It concerns the sketchbook.'

'Yep, I've still got it safely stored.'

'It will mean a little work for you, but I think you'll find it well worth the while and should get your name in front of a lot of cameras and newspapers.'

'Tell me more. I'm all for a bit of fame.' The grin on Simon's face warmed Robert.

'No one alive has seen the sketchbook that you have in your possession other than you and me, and no one knows for certain that it exists, except for two crooks, but they've never seen it, either. So, I've thought long and hard about this during the time I've been in here, and, in hindsight, it's something I should have done ages ago, but had been unable to do so.'

Simon's face showed concern and curiosity.

'Simon, have you looked at the sketchbook? Inside, I mean?'

'Well, to be honest, Robert, I did glance at its contents. It is fabulous. It looks incredibly like Turner's work from the little I know of him and his paintings. Whether or not it is, the sketches are beautiful. Such detail. I didn't know that he had been to Venice.'

Newspaper Man Uncovers Priceless Turner Sketchbook

London, December 1961 - In an astonishing turn of events, Simon Williams, a diligent freelance newspaper man, has unearthed a priceless artifact that has sent ripples through the art world. Williams, 34, discovered a long-lost sketchbook belonging to the renowned English painter, J.M.W. Turner.

The historic significance of this sketchbook cannot be overstated, as it contains previously unseen sketches and studies by Turner from his time in Venice, Italy in 1819, providing new insights into the master artist's creative process.

Williams, seen here holding the precious sketchbook with a mix of pride and reverence, is handing over the treasure to Sir David Reid, General Manager of the Tate Gallery, London. The sketchbook will now reside in one of the country's most prestigious art institutions, where it can be studied and admired by scholars and art enthusiasts alike.

Simon Williams has announced that he will divulge the thrilling details of his remarkable find in a series of upcoming articles in various magazines and Sunday papers starting next week. Readers are eagerly awaiting these publications to learn more about the circumstances surrounding the discovery of this extraordinary artifact.

The art world holds its breath as the story unfolds, promising to illuminate new facets of J.M.W. Turner's legacy and enrich our understanding of one of Britain's greatest artists. Be sure to keep an eye out for Williams' articles as they shed light on this momentous find.

The Mail is also pleased to announce that Mr Williams has agreed to join its staff immediately after Christmas.

Robert smiled as he read the piece, then the others. He wondered whether Rossi or Mulholland would see the article and how they would feel. He didn't want to gloat but their not getting hold of the book gave him a sense of gratification.

As the prison months passed, Robert found a sense of resilience within himself. He learned to endure, to survive, to hold on to the hope that one day, with people like Simon helping to make others understand that homosexuality was not a danger to society, things would change. That one day, love would no longer be a crime, and he and others like him could live their lives in peace.

And so, he waited, counting down the days until he could walk out of the prison gates. A free man.